'What's the pr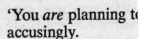

'You *are* planning t
accusingly.

Stefan shook his head. 'No. I'm afraid I don't agree with the idea of seduction. It rather implies that one party at least is less than willing.'

'Do you like your conquests to be effortless?' she taunted.

He raised his eyebrows. 'You make me sound lazy, Ferry, and I can assure you that I am a most attentive lover.'

Dear Reader

This is the time of year when thoughts turn to sun, sand and the sea. This summer, Mills & Boon will bring you at least two of those elements in a duet of stories by popular authors Emma Darcy and Sandra Marton. Look out next month for our collection of two exciting, exotic and sensual desert romances, which bring Arab princes, lashings of sun and sand (and maybe even the odd oasis) right to your door!

The Editor

Jenny Cartwright was born and raised in Wales. After three years at university in Kent and a year spent in America, she returned to Wales where she has lived and worked ever since. Happily married with three young children—a girl and two boys—she began to indulge her lifelong desire to write when her lively twins were very small. The peaceful solitude she enjoys while creating her romances contrasts happily with the often hectic bustle of her family life.

Recent titles by the same author:

BITTER POSSESSION
BLAMELESS DESIRE

CHAPTER ONE

IT WAS a very nice office. Very big, with white walls and a large triple-glazed window, which made the traffic outside appear to be engaged in some sort of a mime show. The furniture was of wood, stained navy and yellow. There was a navy door on one side of the room— which presumably led through to her new boss's office— and a yellow coat-stand on the other side, upon which she hung her raincoat. Having done that, Ferry stood very still and very straight and thought very, very hard. When she had come to her decision she made her way swiftly across to what was to have been her desk, picked up the telephone receiver and dialled.

'Angela?'

'Hi, Ferry! No problems? You *are* going to go, aren't you?'

'I'm already there.'

'But it's only eight. I'm not properly dressed yet.'

'Oh, come on; you know how surprised they always are when they find out what time I start ... Anyway, the bus didn't take as long as I thought it would. But I'm not staying.'

'But Ferry——'

'But *nothing*, Angela. You promised me a travel agency. You absolutely promised. It's the middle of April already, and if I'm to get to Crete before the crowds build up I need to be where the cheap flights are *now*. Not fiddling around with invoices for pepperpots.'

'Pepperpots?'

'Angela, this is not a travel agency. You lied to me.'

5

'I didn't! I simply said that the job was exactly what you were looking for.'

Ferry sighed bleakly. She hadn't wanted to have to make this call. Now that she had done, she wished Angela would just agree with her for once. She was making it even more difficult.

'Lunchtime, Angela. I'll give you till twelve-thirty to find me a job with a travel agency,' she said, making herself frown determinedly, and hoping that by wearing the right expression on her face she could make her voice sound more resolute. 'Any later and I'll take my exceptional speeds to some other secretarial agency, and give *them* the benefit of my unrelenting cheerfulness.'

'But Ferry...'

'Lunchtime. OK?' And the receiver clicked neatly back down on to its cradle. Ferry heaved a sigh of relief. It was not good—she had to have that holiday—and soon. She'd worked it all out and she was sure that if only she could manage a week in Crete, enjoying the sun, seeing the sights, away from the crowds, then things would come right in no time at all. She closed her eyes briefly.

When she opened them it was to find that she was being observed by a tall male in shirt-sleeves who was standing just in front of the now open navy door. A tall and stunningly good-looking male. A male with honey-coloured eyebrows, drawn together into a frown which was anything but honey-coloured.

'Hello,' she said brightly, hoping against hope that he hadn't been there for too long, 'I'm Miss Lyon. From the High-Temp Agency.'

'And you are unrelentingly cheerful?' The words came out in a slow and unbelievably disgusted growl.

Oh, dear. Long enough ... Ferry struggled to readjust her slithering composure. She smiled broadly, revealing her even white teeth. 'I'm afraid so. And you are...?'

'Stefan Redwell. Unrelentingly irritable.' He wasn't being sarcastic this time, either. There was something in the way the deep, resonant voice ground out between clenched teeth which informed her of that fact very convincingly indeed.

Somewhere, deep behind her cheerful smile, she swallowed hard. She was in trouble...

'I must compliment you, Mr Redwell,' Ferry said cagily, 'on the choice of telephone. It was a pleasure to use. Those old GPO phones are just the right weight and shape for comfort, and they don't slip all over the desk, either. What a clever idea to have them converted for modern digital systems.'

'Miss Lyon——' in his voice now was undeniable proof of his earlier assertion of irritability '—you appear to be labouring under the apprehension that I am a fool. You are wrong.'

'Yes, sir.' She blinked very slowly and bit on the inside of her lip. When in doubt, always agree.

'Do you know Angela well?'

'Yes, sir. Since our schooldays, sir.'

'Then you can tell her that I am not a fool, and I will not be taken for one. If you leave now you will arrive back at the agency in plenty of time to find yourself a job with a travel agent by lunchtime.'

Oh, dear. What on earth could she say? Ferry surveyed him submissively, her angular, freckled chin tucked in, her grey eyes looking expectantly upwards beneath her very straight nut-brown fringe. She couldn't deny that she'd brought this embarrassing situation upon herself. Quite honestly, if she had any sense she'd stand up and wave an unrelentingly cheerful goodbye. Right now. In theory, it was exactly what she wanted to do. In practice, she found she didn't like the idea one little bit. How very odd.

'But what will you do for a secretary, sir, if I go?'

'Exactly what I would have done after lunch, I presume.'

Ferry winced. Well, he certainly wasn't a fool. 'Are personal calls not allowed during working hours, sir?' she asked meekly.

He let his cold amber-brown eyes drop to the slim Rolex, nearly buried beneath the dense, dark gold hairs on his wrist. 'Seven minutes past eight. You have *not* made a personal call during working hours. I believe you are due to start work at nine.'

Oh, darn it. That was to have been precisely her argument. 'Er—yes.'

The lion's eyes now fastened themselves very frostily on her wavering gaze. 'But the bus journey was speedier than you had anticipated, and anyway, you wanted to surprise me by turning up early on your first day?'

'Not just my first day, sir. Every day.'

'Really?' The sarcasm was back.

'Yes, sir.'

'God damn it, could you stop calling me sir? It's very annoying.'

'By all means, Mr Redwell.'

'Why on earth do you come in so early? Once for good effect should surely be enough, unless you're hoping to be offered a permanent position.'

She locked her fingers anxiously in front of her silky cream blouse. 'I'm very often offered a permanent position, Mr Redwell. I'm . . . well, actually I'm very good, you see. But I prefer temping.'

'If you're so good why do you have to keep coming in early to prove it?'

'I don't come in early to prove it,' she said honestly. 'I come in early to get a great deal of work done in peace and quiet early in the day when I'm fresh. And then I go home an hour early, unless I'm particularly needed.'

'You do *what*?'

Oh, lord. What did she have to say to this man to put things straight? It was really most dispiriting. Ferry had worked for more bosses than she cared to remember. She had never been wrong-footed by any of them before—or not this seriously, anyway.

'Oh, I don't insist upon it, Mr Redwell, in case you're imagining that I'm a bit uppity for a temporary secretary. It's just that...well, most of my employers find that the arrangement works very well. I make a point of having a completely clear desk by four, and they're usually fading a bit by then anyway, and don't have much for me to do.'

'Fading by four? No wonder you think you're so good, if you've been in the habit of working for mental geriatrics.'

'Do I take it that you go on producing fresh work much later than that, Mr Redwell?'

'Much, much later. And stop calling me Mr Redwell.'

'Certainly, Mr—um——' She hesitated uncertainly, then added more firmly, 'Then it won't prove a very good working arrangement for us, will it? I shall stay as late as I'm needed.'

'That won't be necessary. I should hate to deprive a travel agent of your unrelenting cheerfulness.'

Oh, dear. The meek-and-mild act wasn't working. Oddly enough, the realisation gave Ferry a degree of courage. The more this conversation went on, the less she had to lose—or so it seemed. Probably, she admitted ruefully, because she'd lost it already. But at least she was going down fighting.

Ferry tilted her chin and surveyed him directly with every fraudulent shred of goodwill she could muster pasted to her face. Actually, she was quite confounded by the man. Most men who had attained a position in life which required a secretary were very susceptible to the subservient, upturned gaze, which Ferry, being tall, could only manage when seated. This one wasn't typical, though, in any sense. There was no paunch; no overwhelming waft of middle-priced aftershave. And he was a touch on the young side—mid-thirties at most—to have got himself so bogged down in the business of distributing cruets. No wonder he was irritable.

'Would it make any difference,' she said consideringly at last, 'if I concealed my cheerfulness? Does it bother you that I'm happy? Is that the problem?'

Ah! Progress. His nostrils quivered slightly, as if he might just have allowed himself to be momentarily amused. He was a big man, impressively tall, and his features had a solidity which matched his frame. When she had first looked up to find him standing in the doorway she had decided instantly that he was goodlooking. She let her eyes come to rest on his thick, dark gold hair—whose impeccable styling could not disguise a wilful tendency to curl—and decided that she had modified her opinion. His features were too uneven—too unusual—to be considered classically handsome. But there was something utterly compelling and quite devastatingly attractive about his face with its high cheekbones, and the strong nose, which looked ever so slightly as if it might once have been broken. It was that marginal flattening at the end of his nose which gave the game away. It threw his nostrils into relief, and had drawn her attention to the almost imperceptible flickering of their borders. His tawny eyes, uncannily, had remained quite impassive.

'It's true that I would find your good humour hard to stomach if you were to remain. However, the point is academic.'

Oh, well, that was it. He'd won. Ferry sighed and got to her feet. She made her way across to the coat-stand and unhooked her raincoat.

'Well, I must say that I'm sorry not to have been able to demonstrate my abilities,' she said with a final flash of spirit. 'Now you will always think me a liar—and I'm not. I really am a first-rate secretary. Still, perhaps it makes us quits. After all, I shall now always think of you as unprincipled.'

'Unprincipled?'

'Yes,' she responded, sounding a little more cross than was perhaps acceptable for someone who had so recently claimed to be unrelentingly cheerful. 'You eavesdropped on a private conversation, and then used the information against me. After all, my quarrel was with Angela—not you. And quite justifiably so. She had promised me a travel agency job—and, considering how much goodwill my efforts bring to the agency, I don't see why I shouldn't be able to pick and choose occasionally. I didn't discover the truth until the post came this morning, and by then it was too late. However, I did turn up here—though I could easily have left you in the lurch.'

'Surely Angela wouldn't have tolerated that?'

Ferry bit back the truth, which was that Angela probably would have done—as a one-off, at any rate. She normally never let Angela down—quite the reverse. Angela would have understood. They had been close friends for a very long time now. However, she could hardly say that to Stefan Redwell.

'No. She wouldn't. But I wasn't lying either when I said that I am frequently offered excellent jobs. London is a very big city. I'm not entirely dependent on Angela's goodwill. Anyhow, considering that I was quite prepared to stay on here, despite the pepperpots, I do think you might have been more tolerant.'

His eyes narrowed harshly, but his nostrils were active again. Obviously he wasn't quite as unrelentingly irritable as he liked to make out. 'Miss Lyon——' he began coldly.

But at that moment the telephone console on Ferry's desk began to flash. 'Excuse me a moment,' she interrupted, lifting the receiver. Then, 'Good morning, Mr Redwell's secretary speaking . . .' she said in her best telephone voice. 'How can I help you?'

'Ferry, it's Angela! Look, I know it's not the right sort of business, but just wait till you see the man himself. He's superb—and I've just handed him to you on a plate . . .'

'I've met him already. And you're quite wrong. He isn't at present standing on any recognisable piece of china whatsoever. Though I have to admit I wouldn't mind seeing his head on a salver. Preferably with an orange stuck in his mouth. He's just sacked me.'

'But Ferry——'

'Bye, Angela. See you soon.'

This time when she risked a glance at him he was smiling broadly. His teeth were even and white, and looked exceptionally strong. What with the hair and the nose, and now the teeth, he looked positively leonine. She dropped her eyes in private acknowledgement of the message her stomach had just delivered. When he smiled like that she could see exactly what Angela had meant. He *was* superb. Though he quite clearly wasn't about to present himself to any woman on a plate. Least of all her.

'Take off your coat, Miss Lyon. You may stay. But you'd better be as good as you say you are,' he growled irritably.

'I am,' she murmured demurely. She should have felt relieved—even though she was going to have to postpone her holiday. In fact she felt a good deal more than relieved. She felt unexpectedly exuberant. She slipped her arms out of the sleeves and dropped her coat back on to the hook. 'Thank you. I can promise you won't regret this.'

Something close to contempt marked his features as he considered this remark. 'Oh, but I shall, Miss Lyon. I think we can both be quite confident of that, can't we? But on the other hand I'm hoping that you'll end up regretting my decision every bit as much as I expect to myself...'

Ferry swallowed hard, and to her surprise felt a warm colour creeping up her neck. Stefan Redwell had sounded decidedly threatening—though she could hardly blame him. Ferry herself had been shocked by her own outspokenness. It wasn't her style at all. Something had got into her this morning, obviously, and now she had created a terrible impression with this new boss of hers and would have to work very hard to put things right.

Still, she thought uncertainly, it oughtn't be a problem. She really was very good at her job, and soothing irritable bosses was a skill she had honed to perfection over the years. Except that something seemed to be warning her that Stefan Redwell mightn't be all that easy to soothe...

'Er—I'll try my best to be agreeable, sir.'

'Liar.'

She blinked, and then suddenly and inexplicably felt like laughing, though she managed not to. Formidable he might be, but there was something very exhilarating

about his unpleasantly direct manner. She always claimed
she could stand a fortnight of just about anything. She
was obviously about to be put to the test.

'What would you like me to do?' she asked equably.

'The next room along the gallery houses the coffee-
machine,' he snapped, turning brusquely towards the
navy door. 'I take mine black, no sugar. And be quick
about it.'

Ferry grimaced as he slammed the door behind him.
She must be going round the bend. She had just gone
out of her way to ensure that she kept a job she didn't
even want. Surely it wouldn't have mattered that much
if she'd been sacked just once? Angela probably would
have been sympathetic, and anyway, as she'd said to
Stefan, London was a big place. It could hardly have
affected her future employment prospects at all. But that,
Ferry acknowledged wryly, hadn't exactly been worrying
her, anyway.

She got to her feet. Black coffee, he'd said. And be
quick about it. Now where did he say that coffee-machine
was? Finding everyday essentials like coffee-machines
usually presented her with no problems. But Redwell
House had taken her by surprise. It had a wonderfully
elegant and completely authentic Georgian façade, but
behind it the structure was entirely modern, and,
moreover, built around an atrium containing a fully
mature Scots pine. It was almost as unexpected as the
lion-like Mr Redwell himself, who had failed to live up
to her preconceived expectations in any respect
whatsoever.

''Nature of the business: tableware distribution'', the
agency card had read. The words had conjured up an
image in her mind of elderly waitresses laying up a long
table; spacing out the cruets; distributing the saucers in
which sat forlorn curls of butter, just too far apart for

anyone to reach conveniently. The managing director of such a firm ought to have had a bald spot, a shiny suit and a grizzled moustache which drooped into his coffee-cup. Stefan Redwell had none of those attributes.

Still, however unpredictable boss and building had turned out to be, the coffee-machine was bound to fulfil all her worst expectations. She had, for a start, just *known* there would be a coffee-machine. An inefficient coffee-machine with those wobbly plastic cups, tinted the colour the coffee ought to be but never was. No doubt there'd be a randy warehouseman too, lurking about somewhere, a left-over from the brilliantined Fifties, waiting to give her the glad eye. She eyed the phone indecisively. Should she ring Angela back? Or wait a while?

The coffee-machine was a genuine Italian espresso machine—ornate and gleaming, and, eventually, when she had figured it out, capable of producing the most deliciously aromatic coffee, complete—as far as her own cup at least was concerned—with milky froth. She took his in with an air of supreme confidence. She hadn't been quick, but if she behaved as if she were fleet-foot Mercury himself, then surely he wouldn't notice?

'What detained you?' he asked derisively.

She smiled, nonplussed. He certainly didn't run true to type. Bosses who noticed things like that were, in her experience, miserable, headmasterly men, nearing sixty. There was a renegade cast to Stefan Redwell's features which would automatically have debarred him from obtaining employment in any school in Britain. Or the world. Or the universe, come to that.

'I'm sorry,' she murmured. 'I've never used a machine like that before.'

'Tut-tut,' he returned wryly. 'You promised me the world, Miss Lyon, and yet you're foxed by a mere coffee-machine.'

'You have to admit it's not the usual sort of coffee-machine,' she said brightly.

He raised one eyebrow. 'I shall admit nothing. It depends entirely on what you are used to. Now let's not waste any more time. I've put a pile of letters ready for typing on your desk.'

'I can take dictation accurately,' she murmured. 'There's no need for you to write them out.'

Then it was his turn to smile, his lips tight together, his eyes taunting.

When she got back to her desk, the letters, hastily scribbled and with a lot of crossings-out, looked as if they were in shorthand already. But not a type of shorthand she was familiar with. On closer inspection she found that she did recognise some of the characters after all. There was an upside-down L and a six-legged X which jumped out at her with blood-curdling familiarity. The letters must be addressed to a Russian. Because they were all written in Cyrillic script. No wonder he had smiled.

There were, she reflected dismally as she blew the froth on her coffee to the far side of the cup, three options. She could go and ask him what the hell he thought he was doing, giving her letters to type in Russian. Or Polish. Or whatever. Or she could take the next bus to the High-Temp premises and start phoning round the travel agents. Or, then again, she could somehow, and with great aplomb, present him with a pile of beautifully typed letters in Cyrillic script in record time. She smoothed her neat blue skirt with one hand as she bent to plug in the word processor...

With the help of the manual and a plastic keyboard cover printed with Cyrillic notation Ferry at last managed to produce the unfamiliar letters on the screen. However, it didn't take her long to discover that despite the key-

board cover she still couldn't type his letters properly.
How was she supposed to know if he had made any
spelling mistakes, for a start? She drummed her fingertips on the desk. Think, Ferraleth, she urged. Use
your brains, my girl...

Translation agencies? She knew from experience that
even the best of them would take far too long. This job
had to be done quickly if it were to earn her any Brownie
points with the arrogant Mr Redwell. She took her address book out of her bag, found the number she needed
and dialled.

'Simon? What do you mean it's early? It's three
minutes past nine. You university boffins should try
living in the real world for a change...'

It was nine twenty-six when Simon rang her back, and
nine twenty-nine when she sent off her first fax. Six faxes
and an hour and a half later she knocked on the navy
door.

'Come...'

His thick, wavy hair was furrowed where he had been
running his fingers through it. She wanted to laugh again,
but didn't. It looked so like a mane, all tousled like
that... Stefan Redwell. The King of the Beasts.

'Would you like to check these through before you
sign them?'

He frowned impatiently. 'What on earth are you
talking about?' he muttered, keeping his eyes fixed on
the spreadsheets littering his desk.

'The letters. They're ready.'

Still he didn't look up. 'Do you think you might
manage to address me by name, Miss—er——?'

He was feigning the memory loss. Trying to make it
appear as if she had made no impression on him at all.
Short of being called Miss Piggy, she could hardly have
been blessed with a more memorable name.

'Lyon. Ferraleth Lyon. I'm afraid you asked me not to call you Mr Redwell a little earlier, if you remember.'

'Well, I've reversed my decision. It's OK now and again. Just don't keep saying it all the time.'

'By all means, Mr Redwell. Now if you could just glance at these letters...'

He looked up, scowling. She held them out to him. Still glowering, he took them impatiently from her. He studied them briefly, then looked up again. 'Which agency did you use? They're very good. Fast too. We can put a lot of work their way if the price is right.'

'I didn't use any agency, Mr Redwell. I typed them myself.'

His eyes narrowed in disbelief. 'You mean you speak Polish?'

'Only one of them is in Polish. The others are Russian.'

'You didn't answer my question.'

'I'm sorry, Mr Redwell. I don't, as it happens, speak any foreign language except French. And I'm afraid I'm a bit clumsy with that.'

'Then how did you manage this?' He flicked the edge of the letters with his thumb, producing a sharp clicking sound.

'I took the advice of a friend. I used the fax machine to check out spelling and punctuation with him, and so on. He suggested one or two changes. He assured me that they're only minor, but I'd be grateful if you could spare a moment to read them through and make sure you approve, as I'm not in a position to judge for myself. I hope that was in order?'

Stefan Redwell looked long and hard into her wavering grey eyes. At last he dropped his gaze to the letters and read them. His features remained set in fiercely severe lines, but at a certain point in his reading his nostrils gave the game away. They didn't just quiver this time.

They flared, and stayed flared for a long time. He was laughing; she was sure of it. It worried her. He picked up a gold fountain pen from his desk and bracketed a couple of lines on one letter.

'Type this one again,' he said sardonically. 'And leave out the words I've indicated.'

With the help of the word processor she was back at his side in under ten minutes, with the new copy of the letter. Curse him. She was sure she'd copied the immaculately inscribed fax absolutely perfectly the first time. He was just making changes in order to be difficult.

'That's better,' he said, scribbling his illegible signature on the bottom. When he looked up this time he smiled very broadly indeed. 'Well done,' he added, sounding genuinely impressed.

Her stomach clenched again.

'Who is this friend of yours, by the way?'

'Oh, just someone I know who lectures in modern languages at the university,' she murmured vaguely.

'An old boyfriend?'

Now how had he guessed that? 'Er—no. Just a friend.'

'Don't lie to me, Miss Whatever-it-is Lyon. He's an old boyfriend with a score to settle. You may as well admit it.' His deep voice hummed with amusement.

Ferry bit her lip. 'The name's Ferraleth, actually. And I'm afraid my friend is anything but an old——'

'Oh, please!' he cut in drily. 'We've been getting on so well up until now. Don't spoil it all with mendacity. I must be right. Who else would have slipped a message into my letter reading "Make her type this again so that she doesn't get above herself..."?'

Ferry hesitated for a moment. She'd kill Simon if ever she saw him again. However, determined not to be bested by the beast, she smiled breezily. 'An old employer, as it happens, Mr Redwell. An old employer with a score to settle.'

When she got back to her desk she looked up the word 'mendacity', just to be sure. She was right. It was exactly the same as being called a liar. So why did it somehow feel so very much worse?

CHAPTER TWO

THE warehouseman was a messenger, and he was wearing a grey drill jacket rather than a brown drill coat. But the effect was pretty much the same. 'You're looking cheerful,' he said with a lecherous wink, dumping a large pile of letters on her desk.

'I'm always cheerful,' smiled Ferry.

'I'm Ray. Your little ray of sunshine,' he continued, and waggled his eyebrows suggestively. 'You can call me Mr Fields when you're in a bad mood—which should be most of the time once you get to know his lordship,' and he nodded at the navy door. 'He's a beast...' he continued in a confiding stage whisper.

'I'd already figured that one out. The King of the Beasts, in fact...' she whispered back.

Ray scratched his head. 'King? His mother's supposed to be a princess. Hungarian-style if you know what I mean—but I don't think *he's* in line for any titles...'

Ferry took a deep breath. 'Was there something else you wanted, Mr Fields?'

Ray widened his eyes gleefully. 'Is that an offer Miss—er——'

'Miss Lyon,' sighed Ferry wearily.

'So do you roar, Miss Lyon?' And he laughed at his own joke. Then he asked, 'Don't you have a first name?'

Ferry nodded. 'It's Ferry,' she admitted with resignation, waiting for the next awful joke.

'Across the Mersey?'

She tried to puff a little laugh out of her nose but it wouldn't come. She compensated with a feeble smile.

'Look, Mr Fields, I'm afraid I'm awfully busy. Would you mind...?'

Ray looked slightly nonplussed. He made his way huffily towards the door, before turning and giving her a final, half-hearted wink. She couldn't help feeling sorry for him.

Ferry spent the next half-hour dealing with the incoming mail. Its contents baffled her. Stefan Redwell seemed to have fingers in an awful lot of pies—most of them obscurely connected with metal in some way. None of it made much sense to her, and none of it seemed to be concerned with pepperpots. She often found it difficult to get a grip on a company's business at first, though it would always fall into place sooner or later—usually with the help of her boss. This time she suspected she was on her own.

Stefan Redwell went in and out of his office via the door which opened directly on to the gallery. She heard it slam time without number. They had several brief encounters, during which she smiled and he glowered, but nothing at all was said.

Once, when she heard him bang in, she buzzed him and said, 'There's nothing much in your diary for today. I wonder if we could go through your schedule so that I can block in a few things?'

'Why? Does the sight of an empty page in a diary depress you or something?'

'No. But if an urgent call comes through it might be helpful if I had idea of where to find you.'

'If an urgent call comes through, tell whoever it is that I'm out of the office and you don't know when I'll be back.'

Ferry pulled a face. He really *didn't* seem to be taking his pepperpots very seriously. 'But if it's *really* urgent——'

'If I'm out of the building it means that I don't want to be concerned with whatever's going on inside the building. The messenger is pretty good at tracking me down when I'm in. Lunchtime is the only difficult bit.'

'Perhaps if you could just give me details of your luncheon plans...'

There was a pause. Then Stefan said caustically, 'If you really must know, Miss Lyon, today I shall be eating in the Bacchinalean with the Honourable Miss—er—oh, what the hell is her name? She's a blonde... Something to do with oranges. There's a file on her somewhere.'

'Oranges.'

'Yes. She's one of the Pillington-Smythe girls. The one with the nose... You know. Satsuma? Tangerine...?'

Ferry didn't know, but she could guess. 'Clementine?'

'Good girl. I was about to settle for Kumquat. But I must have been thinking of her hat size.'

'Er—do you think we could come to an agreement to speak in plain English to one another, Mr Redwell?'

There was a pause, and then he said sardonically, 'I thought you claimed to be the perfect secretary? In my opinion it is the job of the perfect secretary to know exactly what I'm talking about without my having to explain myself in *plain* English.'

'Uh-huh. I see,' she murmured equably, trying not to feel dismayed at his evident hostility. 'Do you think we could get back to the diary?'

Stefan Redwell gave a dismissive growl. 'OK. If you insist. Tonight, Miss Lyon...do you need to know which type of orange I shall be peeling *tonight* so that you can put it in my diary? Or does your curiosity begin and end with my lunch-hour?'

'No. Of course not,' she said, startled. She smiled hard at the intercom, hoping that she might be able to send a few good-humoured vibes buzzing through it. She was finding all this sparring very difficult to handle. She wasn't used to being on bad terms with her boss.

'Are you smiling, Miss Lyon?' came his voice, dark with sarcasm.

'Er—yes.'

'Then don't...'

'Very well, Mr Redwell.'

His door opened and closed several more times as the morning progressed. Stefan made no attempt to tell her where he might be going, nor for how long.

At last the inter-connecting door opened, but only Stefan's left arm appeared, naked to the elbow and holding the door wide. 'She's in there. Introduce yourself,' he said to the apparition in yellow which glided into the room. The door didn't close immediately, though. Before that happened, his entire arm came into Ferry's office, closely followed by the rest of him, the whole lot coming to rest against the filing cabinet, one naked forearm folded across the other. Ferry couldn't help noticing that his eyes never left the thoroughbred features of the stunning creature, dressed in an immaculate yellow trouser suit, who had made such a grand entrance and now seemed to have taken up centre stage. Oranges and lemons, Ferry found herself thinking. Stefan Redwell seemed to have a thing about citrus fruits. She smiled brightly.

'Rosa Barton,' murmured the apparition. 'I'm Stefan's *permanent* secretary.' Only her glossy lower lip moved when she spoke. 'I remembered those Russian letters, and thought I'd look in quickly as I was passing... I just *hated* the idea of leaving Stefan in the lurch with whatever the agency managed to dredge up.'

'One was Polish,' said Ferry sweetly. 'And they're all in the post already. You can enjoy your holiday with a quiet mind, Miss Barton—everything's under control here.'

The apparition's beautifully shaped brows jumped upwards. 'Don't tell me you speak nine languages, too?' she said with a little shriek of incredulous laughter.

'I don't,' said Ferry regretfully.

Miss Barton smiled with relief and tossed her ebony curls. 'I'm afraid I'm something of a mongrel, you see... *Eight* great-grandparents, all of different national-ities... All descended from one or other of the royal houses of Europe...'

'*Eight* great-grandparents! Good gracious,' mur-mured Ferry. 'How very extraordinary!'

Rosa blinked haughtily. 'Oh, dear, is that the time?' she said, making not the slightest attempt to look at her watch. 'Must rush. I'll catch up with you later, Stefan, darling. *Ciao*.'

And with that she swept out of the room, leaving Ferry swallowing a smile of grim satisfaction. It had been fun telling Stefan that she'd typed those letters. But not nearly as much fun as it had been telling Rosa Barton. She looked across at Stefan. Stefan's eyes met hers. They were indecipherable. He lifted one eyebrow quizzically, then turned and went back into his own office.

Ferry was frowning as she turned back to her desk. What a very odd encounter. Stefan had been watching Rosa like a hawk. Whereas she had not looked at Stefan once.

The only time he used the inter-connecting door again came just before the witching hour of twelve-thirty. He pushed through the door, half in and half out of the jacket of his grey suit, a wadge of papers in one hand.

'I'm going out for lunch. Two hours at least,' he said curtly, kicking the door closed behind him, and wrig-gling his broad shoulders so that the well-tailored jacket fell into place. He flung open a drawer in the navy filing cabinet, extracted a fat file and dropped it heavily on her desk. 'Make sense of that,' he ordered. 'And make an extract of relevant points in order to assist in drafting a report later. Anything pertaining to the efficiency and profitability of the outfit.'

Work like that was outside her brief. It was on the tip of her tongue to protest that if he wanted a high-powered PA he should pay for one, but she caught them back. No one would give a job like that to a temporary secretary on her first morning unless he or she was extremely anxious to bring her down a peg or two. Ferry had never felt less like being brought down a peg or two in her life.

'Certainly, Mr Redwell.'

His eyes narrowed. 'I thought I told you not to call me that all the time.'

'Exactly how many times per day shall I use your name, Mr Redwell?'

He scrutinised her drily. 'How am I supposed to know? It's not the frequency with which you say it, anyway. It's the way you say it. I don't like it.'

'The way I say it?' she echoed evenly.

'Yes. Correct me if I'm wrong, Miss Lyon, but you think you've got this business of soothing the savage breasts of your bosses down to a fine art, don't you?'

'I . . .' Was he a mind-reader? 'I—er—I have to admit I *have* developed a few techniques for—er——'

'For making absolute wallies believe that you think they're Mr Wonderful?'

'Sort of. But only in a professional kind of way. You know, to make things run more smoothly in the office. I don't—um——'

'You mean you make their coffee and you call them sir all the time, but you don't stroke their fevered brows?'

'No. I mean yes. I mean, I think you've pretty much got the picture.' She sighed. 'Anyway, I can see that *you* don't like being soothed, Mr Redwell.'

'I just told you not to call me that.'

'Oh, yes. I'm sorry. So what shall I call you?'

'You'd better call me Stefan,' he muttered irritably. 'We'll try that for a while and see how it goes.'

'Very well, Stefan.'

He sighed. 'I shall be back at four to inspect this clear desk of yours. Don't discuss that file with anyone else. Oh, and contact Personnel and get them to show you around a bit. Get them to show you our pepperpots.'

She eyed him suspiciously. He was mocking her. 'Exactly what sort of tableware does the Redwell group distribute?' she asked cagily.

'Tableware distribution? Is that Angela's phrase?'

Ferry produced the card from her bag and handed it to him. 'Usually I go into the office and get a briefing. But she said you only told her about the vacancy on Friday night at a party. There wasn't time. I got that in the post this morning.'

He shrugged. 'Typical,' he muttered.

'Has she got it wrong? Don't you distribute—er—tableware at all?'

He gave another dismissive shrug. 'Redwell's is an old business. We've expanded over the years—incorporated a diverse range of firms under the one banner,' he said cryptically, then added, 'Our key installation is a plant in Sheffield making highly specialised steel alloys. Mostly for the aerospace industry these days.'

'Oh,' murmured Ferry, then grinned, nodding at the card. 'That's some typing error. I'll tell her.'

'Oh, no,' he said, his eyes drooping at the corners as if he found all this talk of business very tedious indeed.

'It's not a typing error. This London office deals with tableware all right.'

'Those little plastic knives and forks you get on aeroplanes?' joked Ferry, wondering why he sounded so bored with it all.

He shook his head irritably. 'We also have a fairly big factory in Sheffield which makes high-quality steel and plate cutlery. The sort of stuff you see on sale in velvet-lined boxes in big stores and jewellers. A lot of the marketing and PR work for that side is done down here in London. And we have a commissioning agency fronted by a Bond Street shop. I suspect that's what Angela was referring to. In fact I'm sure of it. *That's* the bit that...ah...distributes pepperpots.'

'Oh. I see.' She didn't, actually, but she wasn't about to say so.

The phone rang just as he was leaving. She picked up the receiver.

'Hi, Ferry? You're still there. I thought you said you'd been sacked.'

'You must have been mistaken.'

'Pardon? Anyway, look, I've got two possibles lined up. Neither of them is a very good job and one's with a bucket shop but——'

'Certainly, sir. I'll pass your message on to Mr Redwell later. You did say it was waste-paper bins you were selling?'

His foot left the door, and it slammed shut.

'Sorry about that, Angela. The new boss turns out to be an eavesdropper.'

'Stefan? An eavesdropper? Oh, come on, Ferry!'

'An eavesdropper and a brute.'

'You don't mean he's been brutish with you behind the filing cabinet already?'

'No, Angela, he has not. Unlike your dear self I actively discourage that kind of fraternisation. You should know me well enough by now. None the less I shall be staying on. He's challenged my abilities. I intend to make him eat his words before I get on with fixing my next holiday.'

Wham. A door slammed. He was on his way back. She dropped the receiver back in its cradle—not quite in the nick of time.

'Still planning your holiday?' he drawled scornfully.

'No. Telling Angela that I shall be staying on here after all.'

'So she's had a sex-change and she sells waste-paper bins now, does she?'

Ferry closed her eyes. 'Sorry,' she found herself saying weakly. The man had got her on the run.

'You're damn well going to need a holiday by the time you're through working here.'

'More than likely,' she conceded through clenched teeth.

'Looking for a steamy holiday romance, are you?'

Ferry's grey eyes flashed. 'That comment was unnecessary and offensive,' she muttered, genuinely furious at last. 'Travel broadens the mind. If your mind were a little broader you'd understand why I'm not interested in a decadent fortnight spent lolling in the arms of a muscle-bound half-wit called Pepe.'

'You don't pronounce it like that.'

'I *know*.'

She glowered at him for a moment, until Stefan let out a short growl of a laugh.

'You're annoyed,' he announced with evident satisfaction. 'I've killed that bloody cheerfulness of yours stone-dead. Good.'

'Congratulations,' she said crossly. 'Do you think you could stop being so unrelentingly irritable now?'

He laughed again. 'Unfortunately, my ill humour has not been devised by a special-effects department. It's a quite genuine and spontaneous manifestation of my underlying mood. And I don't propose doing anything to curb it.'

'That's not fair!' she exclaimed, taking herself quite by surprise. 'I'm genuinely cheerful, too!'

He gave her a very dry smile. 'Not any more, you're not,' he said mockingly.

She frowned. He was quite right. 'In that case, was there something you wanted?' she asked frostily. 'Other than to catch me in the act of using the phone?'

He leant across her and scribbled a phone number on the pad in front of her. 'That's my Sheffield secretary's number. Candice Legrice. I deal direct with her from the phone and fax lines in my office. Whenever I enter or leave the building, let her know.'

Ferry refrained from pointing out that he had already more or less refused to let *her* know that selfsame thing. Never mind. She'd already set up a system for tracking him with the girl on the reception desk. She picked up her phone and began dialling the number, at the same time watching his back accelerate out of the door. He might look like a lion, but he charged about the place like a bad-tempered rhino.

Ferry learned three new things that afternoon. Two of them were discovered before four o'clock, when Stefan returned to inspect her desk.

The first discovery was sufficiently pleasurable to induce her to skip lunch. She learned that a fat file could be as fascinating a read as a good detective novel. Or at least it could when the file revealed through letters—each, fortunately, with a translation attached—the history of a Hungarian silversmith and his ancestors, back through the turbulent years of his country's history to the opulence of the last century and beyond. Reading it was no problem. Extracting the relevant points was a little more trying, given that one's main interest lay in discovering how the silversmith's father met the inspiration of his life and married her in secret in a Bulgarian monastery. The mass of documents pertaining to import and export licences—and visas, and hallmarking restrictions—all interleafed with the letters was positively infuriating.

The second discovery was that pepperpots barely figured in the range of wares distributed by Redwell. The commissioning agency, which the London offices were primarily designed to service, turned out to be a kind of super-jeweller's, bringing together designers and silversmiths and clients in order to produce gilded and jewel-encrusted tureens and cutlery and sauceboats to grace the tables of the super-rich. It was, apparently, extremely famous within certain circles. Ferry, of course, had never heard of it. She was taken to the vaults and shown a selection of items. They were stunningly opulent.

Stefan returned at two minutes to four. He banged first into his own office, and then two minutes later into hers. He glanced at her clear desk.

'What next?' she asked lightly.

'You're hoping I'll say "nothing", and then you can go home, aren't you?'

She sighed. She was, actually. It had been a long day and she was beginning to be seriously worried by her decision to fight for this particular job. She was supposed to be in control of her life, and yet she didn't feel the least bit in control when Stefan Redwell was around. Crete would have helped matters. Stefan Redwell was hindering them.

'Well, that would certainly be very nice. But as you've already informed me that you will want me to work on after four, it would be irrational for me to hope for it, wouldn't it?' she said with a bright smile.

'Rational as well as cheerful,' he muttered disbelievingly, his eyebrows arching so that his high, broad forehead furrowed dramatically. 'Where's the file?'

'On your desk with my comments attached, Stefan.'

His brow descended abruptly into a frown. 'What did you say that first name of yours was again?'

'Ferraleth.'

'How do you spell it?'

She spelt it.

He looked sideways at her through narrowed eyes. 'I can't possibly call you that,' he said.

'You can always call me Miss Lyon as you did earlier,' she suggested.

He shook his head. 'Ferraleth?'

'It's a real name. My mother didn't make it up. If you look in any dictionary of names you'll find it between——'

'I don't doubt it. But I can't use the name.'

'Why on earth not?'

'It's far too beautiful. What do your friends call you?'

Ferry looked piercingly at him with her wide grey eyes. 'Too beautiful? Can I enquire *exactly* what you mean by that? There are many insults I will submit to in the line of duty, but I've a feeling that if you meant what I think you meant I should not let this one pass unremarked.'

The corners of his mouth curled upwards a little, and his nostrils broadened almost measurably. 'So what do you think I meant?'

'I shall reserve comment until you've answered my question.'

He shrugged. 'I simply find the name beautiful. I'd never heard it before, but now that I have I can only compliment your parents on their taste. However, having come to that conclusion, I find I can't bring myself to use the name. It is far too lovely a thing to be bandied about the office like a tennis ball.'

'I thought so,' muttered Ferry, making her own mouth into a straight, disapproving line. 'It's perfectly all right for *me* to be bandied about the office, but not my beautiful name. Very revealing.'

Stefan smiled broadly. 'Are you fishing for a compliment, Miss Lyon?' he suggested acidly.

'Certainly not,' said Ferry stiffly. 'My beauty, as we are both very well aware, does not compare favourably with that of my name.'

He surveyed her with unmistakable amusement glittering in his golden-brown eyes. He didn't contradict her. Not even a token shrug. 'So what shall I call you?'

Ferry blinked once, very slowly. 'You can call me Ferry. For just as long as you find it acceptable for me to be calling you by your first name, that is. The moment you change your mind on that, you can revert to Miss Lyon.'

'Ferry it is,' he agreed lightly, unbuttoning his shirt-cuffs and beginning to roll back his sleeves. He made his way towards the door. 'Get Personnel to send along the application forms of the short-listed candidates. They'll know the ones I mean. Then bring them through to me. You can take some dictation then.'

'Certainly. I shall see to it at once,' murmured Ferry. But once he was out of the room she simply sat still. There had been something decidedly flirtatious underlying his comments about her name. Which was odd, as they both understood that her straight brown bob, neat features, and tallish, slimmish figure did not quite compensate for the fact that she was freckled from top—quite literally—to bottom. Even her lips were freckled. Ferry did not consider her freckles a disadvantage. She liked them. And she certainly never ran short of admirers, most of whom sooner or later referred to her as their little speckled egg. But none of her admirers had been quite in Stefan's league.

Apart from the blue blood coursing in his veins and his arresting, leonine countenance, the man had a sort of sublime confidence which suggested that he never made do with second-best. And, although a speckled egg might be a veritable prize at most men's breakfast-tables, a speckled lady on this man's arm would not be at all appropriate. So why had he flirted with her? So that he could snub her? But he hadn't put her down. *She* had been the one to draw the disparaging inference from what he had said, and there had been something far more congenial and flattering in his tacit agreement than there would have been in a flat and untruthful contradiction. It was as if he had been colluding with her in some mysterious way: as if by agreeing that yes, her freckled face did not match the beauty of her name he was prepared to accept her at her own evaluation—which presumably included her assertion that she was very good at her job.

So he was prepared to concede that she was a very good secretary—even though he had, as yet, only the scantiest evidence? And equally prepared to have her understand quite firmly from the outset that she was not about to be treated brutishly behind the filing cabinet?

It was at this point in her contemplations that Ferry made the third discovery of the afternoon. Which was that she found Stefan Redwell the most astonishingly attractive man she had ever met in her life. The realis-

ation frightened the life out of her. Anxiously, she picked
up the phone and got on with her work.

When she went through to Stefan's office she found
him peering irascibly at her comments on the fat file. It
was clear that he didn't like them. She hadn't really expected him to.

'Sit down,' he said, not lifting his eyes.

She sat.

'You don't seem to approve of our proposals,' he said
scathingly, raising his eyes slowly to challenge her own,
and leaning back in his chair, his hands linked behind
the back of his head.

She nibbled at the corner of her mouth. She was beginning to wish she'd confined her comments on the file
to financial matters. What had got into her today? Still,
it was too late to go back and do it over. She would just
have to take the bull by the horns.

'Not really,' she began, venturing a cheerful smile.
'Not that it's any of my business, and anyway, I couldn't
be less well qualified to comment. I don't know the first
thing about hand-made silverware. But I don't think your
plans are fair to Mr—er—Munkácsy—is that how you
pronounce it? Anyway, the silversmith and his son.'

'And why not? Surely if we were to provide them with
the level of support I am recommending they could have
no cause for complaint.'

'It's a generous idea,' conceded Ferry. 'But I . . . well,
I think you're being absurdly romantic.'

'Romantic?' His voice grated with disdain.

'Yes.' Ferry wasn't exactly sure that she believed in
what she was saying. Finding fault in order to annoy
Stefan had been her only consideration when she had
been reading the file. 'Setting them up with a little factory
and turning them back into a thriving business would
provide a fairy-tale ending for that particular story. . .'

And she pointed at the file. 'And no doubt the father, who is clearly completely obsessed with his family's history of craftsmanship, would be thrilled. But the man must be near retirement age. What about the son? What does *he* think of all this? He's a librarian in a medical school in Budapest, isn't he? Perhaps he's only been humouring the old man, letting him teach him all the old skills in his spare time. Perhaps he hates it all. Will he want to give up his city life and return to the country to make knives and forks, no matter how lavish? Anyway, they must both be dreadfully out of date. From a business point of view I should think it's a very dubious idea.'

'Ha!' exclaimed Stefan. 'As it happens I could start taking orders right now. There's been a tremendous interest in the possibility of their resuming production. Do you realise that the old man's great-grandfather rivalled Fabergé in his day?'

'The old man's great-grandfather is, I take it—um—no longer in the best of health?'

'Well, obviously,' sighed Stefan. 'But our accountant is, and he's delighted. He feels that, properly handled, the whole business would prove an enormous money-spinner.'

'Oh, well. If you're only interested in the happy ending as a marketing ploy then undoubtedly you're on to a winner. I still think you ought to find out a great deal more about the son, though, before you go any further.'

'You're a very opinionated young woman, Ferry, aren't you?' growled Stefan.

'Yes,' she returned defiantly. Actually, she had never thought of herself as opinionated, but as she certainly seemed to be behaving as if she was she could hardly deny it.

'Then why, may I ask you, did you elect to become a secretary? Surely it's a most unsuitable job for someone incapable of saying yes, and very wearing for the person they end up working for. Women aren't exactly debarred from more vocal pursuits, these days.'

'I'm a temporary secretary, not a permanent one.'

'Does that make a difference?'

'Yes. It means I can take as many holidays a year as I can fit in. And as it happens I'm quite good at saying yes in the short term. Up until now, that is. In fact I've made a successful career out of *not* irritating all my various employers. But then, most of my temporary employers don't fling important files at me on my first morning and ask me to extract vital information. You will find that all of the requisite information on the financial side has been properly noted.'

'Are holidays the only thing that matters to you?'

'No.'

'I thought you claimed to be good at saying yes.'

She sighed despairingly. 'I *am*. But most of my employers don't——'

'I'm not most of your employers, Ferry.'

'No.'

'Are you ready to take dictation?'

'Yes.'

'Ha! Progress. Then off we go...' And off he went.

He must save a fortune on phone bills, Ferry observed, if he always spoke that fast.

At five-thirty, when she settled down to begin typing the report, her stomach reminded her that she hadn't eaten. She picked up the phone and arranged for something to be done about it.

Ray Fields brought a sandwich to her desk.

'Still happy?' he asked.

'I'm always happy.' She smiled brightly. 'Always. Thank you for going out for this for me, Mr Fields. Can I ask you again?'

Ray winked leeringly. 'You can ask me any time, Miss Lyon...'

She took a deep breath. She knew from experience that there was only one way to put a stop to this. The sooner she got it over and done with the better. 'Why, thank you, Ray,' gushed Ferry, offering him a broad wink of her own in return. 'I was hoping you'd say that.'

He looked decidedly shocked as he scuttled away.

At six-forty Stefan reappeared. This time he was unrolling his shirt-sleeves, and had his jacket slung over one shoulder. 'Time to go home,' he said.

Ferry nodded her acknowledgement, and began shutting down the word processor. She was not fool enough to attempt to impress him any further with her industry. Anyway, she was tired.

He propped himself on the edge of her desk and smiled a smile of unremitting charm at her. 'Come for a quick drink with me,' he said surprisingly.

She felt her heart start to pound with...with fear? 'No, thank you, Stefan,' she replied, keeping her eyes on the screen. 'I've told you already that I don't stroke fevered brows.'

He sighed irritably. 'Ferry, if my brow needed stroking, I'm damned sure you'd be the last person on earth I'd invite to do it. I would *not* find it soothing.'

'Oh,' she said with an uncertain frown. 'So why did you ask me?'

'Because I wanted to see if you were as irritating out of the office as you are in it,' he said. He looked at her steadily for a moment, and then stood up and slipped on his jacket. He strode towards the door and banged out without saying goodbye.

Ferry stuck out her tongue at the receding image. She stretched. Time for the long bus ride home.

CHAPTER THREE

FERRY sat on the upper deck of the bus. She always did, although lately the fact that it seemed to be so much of a routine perturbed her. Would she still be riding home from work on the upper deck twenty years from now? Her heart sank. Something was going seriously wrong with her life. It had become orderly and routine and dispiriting, and she was finding it harder and harder to keep cheerful. The trouble was, she had decided on temping in the first place because it would give her lots of freedom and the chance to meet all sorts of different people in all sorts of different locations. And yet, the more time went by, the more her working life seemed to be settling into a predictable rut all of its own. Was that why she found Stefan so attractive? Because he, at least, was confounding her expectations.

She conjured up an image of his face. The high cheekbones, the thick, golden hair, the amber eyes, alternately taunting and lazy. A fuzzy sensation tickled her skin, making her squirm within the folds of her beige raincoat. She really did find him most attractive, and *that* was the most surprising thing of all. Because Ferry, although she'd had plenty of dates with men she liked very much, couldn't remember ever having been attracted by a man's physical appearance before. In fact, she'd only fallen in love once in her entire life, and then she'd been fourteen and had had fixed braces on her teeth. The braces had precluded any kissing, which Graham Sheen, being rather shy, had not seemed to mind.

Since then she had dated men on the basis of personality alone. And they'd all kissed her, although no kiss had ever turned her to molten lava in the way it was supposed to do. And unfortunately, no matter how intelligent and pleasant the man had seemed before the kiss, afterwards things always seemed to go wrong. Either their egos would be so bruised by the fact that she clearly found their embraces tedious that they would disappear from her life, or they would stick around, but they would start saying and doing extremely pompous things. This always made Ferry feel desperately sorry for them. It also meant that *she* would soon disappear from *their* lives.

For a very long time it hadn't seemed to matter. But lately, what with her work seeming so predictable, and her girlfriends all seeming to be wrapped up in either high-powered careers or the men of their dreams, Ferry was having to fight a very nasty sinking feeling which kept settling in the pit of her stomach. She had been so determined always to be happy in life. She was still happy, but she had a horrible feeling that it wasn't going to last. And she didn't know what to do about it.

The image of Stefan appeared in her mind's eye again, his shirt-sleeves rolled back, his waistcoat unbuttoned, his eyes regarding her scathingly. She swallowed hard. He couldn't stand her, but it didn't alter the fact that she really was enormously attracted to him. She gave a shiver of pleasure. Would it be possible for her to fall in love with this man? It would certainly be a waste of time, and would undoubtedly prove painful. But surely it had to be better than sitting on the tops of buses, looking down on all the seething life in the street beneath, and forcing herself to feel cheerful, no matter what...

Back in her flat, she found she was still pondering the question when she plopped gratefully into her bath. She'd never actually tried to fall in love before. She'd just imagined it was something that would hit you, out of the blue. But Stefan—despite the fact that he didn't like speckled eggs—had stirred her in a way that no other man had ever done. She was convinced it could be done, and surely there would be no harm in it?

He was in before her the next morning. She could hear him whistling tunelessly in his office when she plugged in the word processor at three minutes past eight.

She opened the door to his office. 'Coffee?' she asked.

'Hnngg...' he said, a pencil clenched between his teeth, his eyes fixed on a graph spread across his desk.

When she brought him his coffee he still didn't look up, but one big hand, the back sprinkled with wiry golden hairs, reached out and picked up the cup from the desk. He brought it to his mouth in a wide arc, taking care not to let the cup hover over the papers on his desk, and sipped noisily.

'Too hot,' he said, his eyes at last flicking up to acknowledge her.

They glinted amber in the morning sun. Ferry swallowed hard and made herself look away. The cup clashed back down on to the saucer.

'Could you tell me a bit more about the business?' she asked brightly in an attempt to distract herself from the sight of those big hands of his unbuttoning the cuffs of his bold blue and white striped shirt. An image had just flashed unbidden across her mind of those selfsame hands unbuttoning the buttons of her green silk blouse. Oh, dear... He rolled back his sleeves. The sunlight streaming in through the window caught the hairs which coated his muscular forearms, so that they seemed to hover over his tanned skin in a golden fuzz. Now she was imagining herself bending across the desk and running her lips very lightly up and down his arms, so that the gilded tips prickled against her skin. She ran her tongue over her lips. She had never, *ever* imagined such things before. And had never felt the sort of feelings that came with such thoughts. What on earth was the matter with her? Was this how it felt to fall in love?

'Why? Do you dabble in the stock market?'

The question brought her back to earth with a jolt. 'No.'

'Then you're not planning on a little insider trading? So why do you want to know?'

'Er—well . . . I work here.'

He shrugged. 'Only for a couple of weeks.'

'Yes. But surely if I were better informed——'

'What?' His head butted forward, and one hand came up to push a lock of hair back from his high, broad forehead. 'You mean you'd be an even *more* perfect secretary if only you were better informed?' he said incredulously. His eyebrows shot up. 'What are you trying to do, Miss Lyon? Wangle yourself a permanent job here? Insinuate yourself so immaculately into the scheme of things that you become indispensable?'

'Not at all. I simply thought——'

'You *thought* when you arrived yesterday that we were in the business of moving pepperpots from A to B. And, put crudely, that is *exactly* what we do. I take it that skinny lad from Personnel showed you some of our stuff?'

'Yes.'

He shrugged again. 'So you know what our pepperpots look like now. What more could you possibly need to know?'

'Well, for instance, if I knew——'

'You don't need to know anything else because, when it comes down to it, there isn't anything else *to* know. However, there are a few things *I* need to know. Like the surname and telephone number of a certain young lady I met at a club last night. Are you any good at research, Ferry?'

'Brilliant.'

'Excellent. Somewhere in Rosa's—your—office is a *Burke's*. You can start there. Her father's older brother is Lord—um—somewhere-in-Devon-with-a-castle. And *Who's Who*, too. Look in *Who's Who*. Her mother's sister writes books about her travels with a donkey in the Western Isles—I can remember her telling me that at about two in the morning. You should be able to track her down given all that information. When you've figured out who she is give her a call and fix her up for lunch with me one day this week. Book a table at the Bacchinalean.'

'What's her Christian name?' asked Ferry evenly, managing to keep the acid out of her voice.

He looked blankly at Ferry for a moment and then threw back his head and let out a great guffaw of laughter. 'I can't remember,' he admitted, and the skin around his eyes crazed with mirth. 'Hang on . . . Angela was there with that guy she's got herself engaged to. *She* might know. Ask her. She's got long black hair and a little mole just there . . .'

'I'm on my way,' muttered Ferry, making briskly for the door. Any minute now he'd start describing her voluptuous figure, and she really didn't want to be around when that happened. Enough was enough.

The girl's name turned out to be Belinda Cholmondeley. She also sounded as if she only moved her lower lip when she spoke. And she sounded slightly miffed at the idea of a mere secretary being a party to her forthcoming date with Stefan Redwell. But not miffed enough to turn him down.

An hour later he demanded more coffee. 'Not so hot this time.'

'Espresso coffee is made with steam. Steam is formed when water reaches a hundred degrees centigrade. I cannot change the laws of physics.'

'Really?' he asked sardonically. 'So there are limits to your abilities? You do surprise me.'

This time it had only required the sound of his voice on the intercom to set her senses buzzing. Her heart thundered and her palms felt moist as she waited for the machine to do its whooshing and wheezing. She turned over a cup and looked at the bottom. Mason's Ironstone. Classy. It felt balanced in her hand, and good to drink from. The perusal of the cup didn't slow her heart-rate, though.

When she took his coffee through he said, 'Rosa always gets it the right temperature.'

'Perhaps Rosa blows on it for you?' She smiled sweetly. His returning smile was anything but sweet. It doubled her heart-rate.

Ferry sat at her desk for a moment, pondering. She certainly found him attractive. But she definitely wasn't falling in love with him. He was so rude to her, for a start. That heavy, sinking feeling seeped back into the pit of her stomach. She rubbed anxiously at the bridge of her freckled nose. Did it really matter that he loathed her? After all, it wasn't as if she wanted him to return her affections or anything...

She picked disconsolately at the edge of her rubber. She had worked so hard keeping cheerful over the years. Yet recently she had started drifting further and further into this awful kind of detached limbo, and it was frightening her to death. She must try harder to fall in love with Stefan. It would undoubtedly hurt. But even hurting had to be better than growing empty and cold inside. Ferry shivered.

Letting her mind run on like this was just making her feel worse. She stood up and made her way briskly towards the door, hooking her hair behind her ears and donning her brightest of smiles. She'd collect the post. The exercise would do her good.

Ray was sorting through the letters in the post-room behind the reception desk.

'Thank you. At least it saves my legs one trip,' he said.

'You're welcome.' She smiled breezily. 'A job like this must be hard on the feet.'

Ray nodded. 'I've got bunions,' he admitted. 'They throb something awful at times. The missus says I should get a sitting-down job, but it's not easy to make a change at my time of life.'

Ferry shot him a sympathetic glance before dipping her head to smile discreetly behind her jaw-length hair, which, being so straight, swung forward on demand like a curtain. Good. She had obviously succeeded in frightening him off yesterday. Now they could talk together properly, like ordinary people, without Ray feeling he had to impress her with his manliness all the time. Why did men do it? Didn't they realise that they were far more impressive when they stopped setting out to impress? Which could be the reason, when you came to think about it, why she found Stefan so attractive. He wasn't trying to impress her at all. He didn't think she was worth the effort.

An hour later the door of his office slammed as he went out of it. Eleven minutes later the door of her own office slammed as he burst through it.

'Why are you always smiling like that?' he asked suspiciously, pacing towards her desk, and leaning forward on it, his arms straight, taking his weight on his knuckles.

'Because I'm always happy. You discovered that yesterday.' He looked very lionish like that, a lock of his thick hair flopping over his forehead, his head slightly forward as if ready to pounce. Was there a hint of pomposity in his posture? No. There was something far too unselfconscious in the way he charged about the place. He wasn't leaning over her like that for effect, that was for sure.

He snorted. 'If that's true, and I doubt it, then it's almost pathalogical. Have you ever consulted a psychiatrist about it?'

'No. It's not an illness, I'm cheerful by choice,' she replied, deliberately ignoring his challenging manner.

'You mean it's like being a vegetarian?'

Ferry looked at him in surprise. None of her previous bosses had ever bothered to enquire about her state of mind. They invariably liked the fact that she was good-humoured—unlike Stefan who rather gave the impression that he would prefer her on the grumpy side—but rarely commented. They seemed to take her equability for granted.

'Yes. I suppose so,' she said. 'I mean, I thought about it—all the pros and cons and so on—and then made up my mind to be happy forever.'

'Nauseating. It makes you sound like some kind of latter-day Pollyanna.'

'Oh, I'm not like her. She made herself feel glad about all kinds of awful things. I don't do that. If something's bad, I certainly confront it. It's just that I *refuse* to let life drag me into the mire of despondency.'

'The mire of despondency...' he growled scathingly. 'How very dramatic.'

'Actually, most people who live their lives in the mire of despondency *are* terribly dramatic about it. You must have noticed. They wail and gnash their teeth about all sorts of things. The cost of their mortgage, and the fact that the housework gets on top of them, and the lack of funds for a month in the Caribbean to put it all right... Surely you know people like that?'

'So?'

'So unlike them I recognise that there are limits to my life and I squeeze the maximum possible out of them. It keeps me cheerful. It's a sort of formula, if you like.'

'What an uninspiring philosophy...'

'It works for me,' she said, trying not to sound cross. 'I'm not evangelising.'

'Absolute garbage.'

Ferry forced a convincing smile.

Then his head butted forward a few more inches. 'What sort of limits?' he persisted.

So he really did want to know? Ferry couldn't help but be pleased. It was so very important to her, and yet nobody ever seemed to take it seriously. Not even Angela.

'Oh...you know. Financial, for a start. And time— there isn't time in life to do *everything*. You have to choose. It's the same with friendships... I just sort of make sure that I know what my priorities are, always, and set about getting the best out of what's there, and resigning myself to the bits that get left out...'

'So how did you get to be so...ah...*wise* at so early an age, Ferry?' he asked with manifest sarcasm.

'I worked it out from observing my mother put up her Christmas decorations.'

'This gets worse...' He groaned and closed his eyes.

Ferry chewed her lip. She felt bitterly disappointed. Well, he'd asked and she was damned well going to tell him. He had no right to be so disparaging about something which was important to her. No right at all.

'She brought me up single-handedly, you see. One year she saw that the tinsel had got all tatty and it bothered her. And I realised that tinsel only exists in order to give pleasure—and yet my mother had let it upset her...'

He was watching her with an unnerving intensity, and Ferry suddenly felt distinctly unnerved. 'I just vowed that I'd never let life get to me in the same way,' she finished lamely.

'Isn't your mother happy?'

Ferry sighed heavily. 'Yes, as it happens she is. And so am I. Only more so.'

'So this philosophy actually increases your level of happiness? You mean you get happier and happier as the days go by? Which date do you think you'll actually burst with it, Ferry? Can you give me advance warning? I'll book the carpet-shampooing firm...'

'Why are you being so rude?' Ferry was taken aback by the sound of her own voice. She wasn't used to hearing herself sound dismayed.

He suddenly gave one of his disarmingly broad smiles. 'Because I'm testing out your claim to be the ideal secretary, Ferry. Perfect secretaries should never lose their cool with their bosses, should they? Anyway, I'm curious about this dreadful compulsion of yours to be happy all the time.'

He'd won. She wasn't going to go on arguing with him. It was far too important to her, and she'd never convince him, anyway. He'd only make her look an even bigger fool if he did succeed in making her lose her temper. She shrugged. 'Point taken,' she said with one of her more vapid smiles.

'I think life must have been very kind to you if you find that being happy is so simple a matter,' he responded sardonically, straightening up and punching his hands into his trouser pockets.

She let out her sigh of relief silently so that he wouldn't notice. How on earth her mouth had kept going when his face had been so close to her own that she could see each bristle on his freshly shaven chin she really didn't know. She felt quite shaky.

'If you say so...' she murmured compliantly.

'Now why are you agreeing with me about that?'

'What good could it possibly do to disagree?' she asked evenly.

Stefan was surveying her now with an expression of almost palpable disbelief in his eyes. He said, 'You're wasting my time, Ferry. I came in here to work. Not to discuss the meaning of life. Where's that report you were typing last night?'

'On your desk.'

'When the hell did it arrive there?'

She glanced at her watch. 'You were out of your office for eleven minutes some seventeen minutes ago. I put it there then.'

He moved towards the inter-connecting door, his back to her. 'Just because you're so good at your job doesn't mean that you can waste my time with useless chatter. Keep your answers to my questions briefer in future, Ferry.'

'Yes.'

Unless she was much mistaken he'd just eaten his words. Which was the point at which she'd promised Angela she'd be walking out. But Ferry wasn't going anywhere, least of all in search of another job. And there was nothing in the decision that was either particularly rational or cheerful.

The door to his office banged incessantly all morning as he toed and froed. Couldn't the man sit still? What

on earth was the matter with him? She found it peculiarly
distracting, because every time he went out of his office
she found herself hoping that he'd come into hers. But
he didn't. Was she just a tiny bit in love? How did one
tell?

That afternoon she minuted two small meetings and
one big one, and spent in total three and three-quarters
hours in his presence. When her eyes weren't glued to
her pad she sneaked glances at him. The broadside view
afforded by her seat allowed her to study his profile in
some depth. The slightly crooked nose, the strong curve
of his jawline and the solid high forehead were already
familiar. The well-contoured mouth proved much fuller
seen from the side than it had appeared face to face.
There was something almost voluptuous in its curves. In
fact, there was something altogether voluptuous in the
way she was allowing her eyes to linger on it. Any minute
now she'd start drooling.

She refocused her eyes and began to take note of his
mannerisms instead—the way his head thrust forward
when his attention was captured, and the endless rumpling of his corn-ripe hair by his big square fingers. His
body language spoke of a man who achieved what he
wanted without needing to resort to cunning or devious
practice. She had no doubt by the end of the afternoon
that he was a very, very formidable man indeed. She was
finding him more attractive by the minute. But she still
hadn't managed to fall in love with him.

Afterwards he sauntered into her office where she was
busy deciphering her shorthand and propped one solid
haunch on the edge of her desk. Ferry raised a hand to
unhook her hair from behind her ears, letting it drop
forward to shield her face. She had just registered that
his bottom didn't squidge outwards when he sat down.
The bulk which filled those well-cut grey trousers was

all solid muscle. She sucked both her freckled lips inwards and bit down on them, trying hard not to laugh. Fancy her, Ferraleth Lyon, noticing a thing like that! Angela was always on about the physical attributes of the men she dated. Ferry had believed it an affectation. *She* barely noticed the colour of the sweaters her dates wore, let alone wasted time dwelling on the contents. And yet here she was, her eyes transfixed by a piece of broadcloth, and her skin buzzing with anticipation as she imagined the bone beneath the muscle beneath the skin beneath the clothes.

'You must be tired,' he said.

'Not really.'

'I am,' he sighed. Then he frowned at her. 'You *must* be. You've been stuck in those meetings for hours, too. You don't have to prove to me how invincible you are any more, you know. I'm quite convinced. You can admit to the occasional weakness.'

Ferry couldn't help the smile of pleasure which broke on her lips. He really was being very nice, for once. 'Thank you! But actually I'm really not tired at all. You've been talking almost non-stop for three and a half hours. I've just been listening. It's much less stressful.'

He screwed up his eyes and rubbed his hands over his face. 'Then if you really aren't tired, Ferry,' he said, 'you can run out and get me a sandwich. I'm bloody ravenous.' And with that he removed his person from her desk and marched back to his own office.

Ferry got Ray to do the running out. This had all gone far enough. Just because she found the man attractive she was allowing her brain to soften. Not cunning, indeed! Ha! A little sympathy and understanding was a classic ploy when it came to getting secretaries to act as waitresses. While she waited for the sandwiches to appear she typed up the first lot of minutes at a furious pace, and had them ready for him when she took in his snack.

'How did you manage that so quickly?' he asked in surprise.

'I got Ray to go out.'

He scratched his chin, giving her an amused look. 'Good lord, Ferry. Don't tell me that Ray's struck lucky at last?'

Ferry felt herself colour hotly. 'Absolutely not.'

Stefan laughed. 'Most of the girls around here won't give him the time of day. We've been considering reviewing our policy on sexual harassment where he's concerned.'

Ferry blinked. Ray had stirred her sympathy, and she couldn't help but jump to his defence. 'You mean you're planning to sack him just because he conforms to type? How many other male employees have you sacked for the same reason?'

'None. But we don't get complaints about the others.'

Ferry humphed. 'Well, I refuse to believe it's because they're all spotless. That squat guy in the pink shirt this afternoon—you know, the one who kept going on about exchange rates in Europe? I'll bet he has a good chat-up line for practically every girl he meets.'

Stefan peered at her. 'Mark? He's a very clever——'

'Quite. Far too clever to wink and make openly suggestive remarks in the present climate. But that doesn't mean that he's not one of life's womanisers all the same. Ray is just too dumb to realise that times have changed. He's quite harmless, you know. He's frightened to death of women in reality. Anyway he has terrible bunions——'

Stefan broke in with a short laugh. 'You mean just because he has bunions he must be harmless? They don't render men impotent, you know.'

Ferry's blush intensified ... She made an exasperated noise with the tip of her tongue. 'It means his feet hurt and he knows he's getting older. I doubt he'd enjoy being dismissed for something like that at his time of life. If you had a quiet word with him and explained that women's expectations in the workplace have changed since he was a teddy-boy I'm sure he'd tone things down immediately. Save your policy review for Mark. You may never have had a complaint about him, but I'll bet he has a high turn-over of secretaries.'

Stefan frowned. 'Ferry, that's a scurrilous thing to say, you know. Unless you've got some evidence ...'

Ferry was feeling distinctly unsettled. 'I've worked for over a hundred men in the last six years,' she muttered defensively. 'I don't need evidence. My instincts are well-honed.'

Stefan's eyes narrowed. 'I shouldn't think sexual harassment would be a problem for you, anyway, Ferry. I'm sure you could frighten ninety-nine per cent of the male population to death with just a single smile.'

Ferry felt herself colouring again. The remark had wounded her. Ferry liked people—men included, even if she did usually end up feeling sorry for them—and she had never had any reason to doubt that they liked her. It was *this* man who was the problem. He was making her behave belligerently. And she wasn't really like that at all. Was she?

'Check with Personnel,' she replied stiffly. 'If I'm wrong I'll take back every word.'

He looked annoyed for a moment, then coolly turned his eyes downwards to his desk and began to read through the minutes. 'There are a couple of spelling errors here,' he said frostily. 'Go back and do it again.'

He was angry with her. For defending Ray or attacking Mark? Or simply for speaking her mind? Ferry never normally spoke her mind in front of her temporary employers. It hardly seemed worth it. After all, she would be moving on... So what had induced her to do it this time? Was it annoyance at that quip he'd made about Ray? She wasn't up to *his* standard, but she'd do for the messenger? And yet he'd made the remark in jest. She'd known that it was only a joke... All of a sudden Ferry had a horrible feeling that she was beginning to lose her sense of humour. All this ogling Stefan was going to have to stop. It was doing things to her personality which she didn't like at all.

Luckily Gerry, her latest swain, took her mind off Stefan for the evening. Gerry was a barrister and very funny, and, better yet, had given up trying to kiss her after about the fourth date.

The next day Stefan had to go to Sheffield, so that was all right. And the following day he was in Amsterdam for a morning meeting, back for lunch with Belinda, and out of the office for the greater part of the afternoon. When he was in the office she managed not to ogle him. Or, at least, almost managed it. The break from his threatening presence gave her a chance to regain her cheerful demeanour.

Friday was a busy day. Towards the middle of the afternoon he buzzed her again. 'Come through for a moment,' he said distractedly.

She went through. He was sitting on his desk, reading a balance sheet, his fingers combing through his hair. When she cleared her throat he looked at her as if he couldn't work out who she was for a moment. Then he said brusquely, 'Cancel whatever you've got on this evening. Then go out and get your hair done and buy a dress. I need you with me at a dinner this evening.'

Ferry pulled a face. 'That's quite irregular...'

He hissed sharply with annoyance. 'Is it? I'll pay double time and of course you can charge the hair and the frock to the firm. But I must have someone with me to get a few things in writing.'

'Why? Can't it wait till the morning?'

'If it could wait till the morning, don't you think I'd let it wait till the morning? Do you think I want to spend my evening stuck in some hotel with this year's Miss Unrelenting Cheerfulness and a bunch of boring bureaucrats from Brussels? Of course I don't. Which reminds me...' And he stood up and went round to his chair where his jacket had been carelessly dumped, and rummaged in an inside pocket. He produced a folder with a couple of theatre tickets in it. 'Arrange for these to be returned... and ring... hang on a moment...' A little more rummaging and he produced a phone number. He scrawled a name beside it. 'Ring this number and tell her I won't be able to make it this evening. Apologise.'

Ferry gave him an old-fashioned look. 'Don't you think it might sound better coming from you?' she muttered haughtily.

Stefan's brow puckered for a moment, and then his eyes hardened. 'No. You do it.' And then he came around the desk and cuffed her lightly between the shoulder-blades. 'You don't have a very high opinion of men, do you?' he asked.

Ferry almost jumped out of her skin. She was burningly aware that although the contact had been minimal he was still standing within inches of her. And suddenly her heart was drumming, her mouth dry, and she could feel that sweet warmth sugaring her skin.

'Er—actually I'm not as hard on them as I suspect I ought to be,' she said scathingly. And she plucked the piece of paper with the number and name on it from his fingers, taking care not to touch. 'After all, I'm about to ring this number for you, aren't I?'

He shook his head slowly, his eyes raking over her. 'You think I'm a roué, don't you, Ferry? Oh, don't bother to answer, it's written all over your face. And you don't think I take my work seriously, either. Does it ever occur to you, Miss Lyon, that you have a very miserable view of the world?'

'I...but I...'

'I know. Don't tell me. You are unrelentingly cheerful and biliously happy.'

As she hurried out of his office he called drily, 'Have a nice day!'

When she studied the scrap of paper back in her own office she felt a fool. The name was Maria Redwell. It was probably his granny or something.

It was his mother. She was staying at Claridge's, and she spoke perfect English with the most mellifluous of central European accents. This was no surprise. Ray had already filled Ferry in on Stefan's background. Mother Hungarian; came to Britain in the mid-Fifties; reputed to be a princess of some sort. Father British; typical top dog of old-established family firm. Mansion with salmon fishing and deer park near Sheffield. Two younger sisters and a brother still at school. Father deceased two years since. Mother something of a merry widow since the unhappy event.

His mother was utterly charming and clearly very disappointed. Ferry suddenly felt very cross with Stefan for not making the call himself. She wished now that she had agreed with him that yes, he *was* a roué and a dilettante.

'Shall I put you through to him?' she asked.

'I...oh, yes...it would be wonderful to hear my darling István's voice...'

'István?'

'Hungarian, you know, my own, precious name for him. Oh, you probably think I'm such a silly, and he is so busy, I know, but we mothers... You must forgive us for our devotion to our children...we are all the same...'

Not all, thought Ferry as she dumped the call on Stefan. Not mine, for instance.

She sat back in her chair and looked at the skyline beyond the window. The sky was bright blue. Apple-green leaves were appearing on the shivering fingers of the trees visible from her desk. A miserable view of the world? He *had* to be wrong. That sinking feeling hit her stomach with a thud. Except that he was right. But how had it happened, and what on earth could she do about it? She could book the holiday in Crete, but she clearly couldn't fall in love. And she knew with a horrible certainty that the holiday wasn't going to be enough.

He barged into her office half an hour later. 'Why are you still here?' he snapped. 'You're not being stubborn, are you? You *are* coming tonight.' This last comment had the air of a statement rather than a question.

'Yes, I shall come.'

'Then what are you waiting for?' He glared at her, then sighed. 'Oh. Arrangements. I would have rung you at home about all that. It's in the banqueting-room at the new Magna Carta. I'll pick you up about eight. OK?'

'I'll get a cab... But that's not why I'm still here. I'm working till five. That's my official finishing time.'

He scowled, looking her up and down. 'You're not coming dressed like that? Hair and dress, I thought I said.'

Ferry found herself colouring swiftly. Good God, he really thought she was a complete sour-faced old frump, didn't he? He thought she'd turn up for a banquet in an expensive hotel dressed in a plain skirt and a neat blouse, just as she did for work. He thought she didn't know any better. 'What exactly would you suggest I do with my hair?' she asked grimly. 'Have it dyed red?'

He stared at it as if he'd never seen it before. 'I don't know, do I? There's not much else you can do with hair like that, is there? Just go to the hairdressers and have it done the same way, I suppose.'

Ferry felt anger fevering up inside her like frantic water in a pan. Her hair, being thick and silky and very, very straight, repaid good cutting. Once a month Ferry went to a superb and extremely expensive stylist and had it cut. In between there was nothing that *could* be done to it except to wash it. She had good hair. She had a good cut. It was always shiningly clean. She had been complimented on it time and again. Why was it good enough for everyone in the world except him?

'So if there's nothing that can be done with it, why do I need to go to the hairdressers for goodness' sake?'

'Because,' said Stefan aggressively, his head butting forward, his eyes glittering, 'that's what women do before they go anywhere.'

'I'm sorry,' she returned sarcastically. 'I didn't realise. I've obviously been deluding myself all these years, believing I knew what I was up to. I hadn't realised that you were such an expert on women, or I'd have come to you for advice sooner.'

'Damn it, Ferry, what's got into you today?' he growled fiercely. 'What's happened to your unrelenting cheerfulness?'

'I took your advice,' she jeered. 'You seemed to think it wasn't such a good idea to be happy all the time, so I've changed my attitude! To hell with your expectations.'

'Well, I don't like it. Whatever I may think of your crackpot ideas about how to live life, that smile at least made you predictable. We're going to be working together this evening whether we like it or not. So get back into cheerful mode right now and go and buy a dress.'

'I have a dress. I don't need to buy one.'

'The firm's paying, for crying out loud. It's a bonus! Get yourself a designer whatnot. Look, I'll ring Rosa and ask her to go with you if you like... She's really well up on——'

'*Shut up!*' Ferry's temper had boiled right over. Oh, this was the living end. He was going to get his cut-glass, top-drawer, multilingual secretary to buy her a *dress*! She almost choked with indignation. She had five work skirts. One for each day of the week. Each one of them was a different plain colour. Each one had been expensive enough. To anyone who understood such things they spoke of cleverly understated elegance. But to Stefan bloody Redwell with his vault full of sapphire-studded silver pudding basins they just looked drab. It would serve him right if she turned up at the restaurant wearing a sack. In fact, she might just do it.

Too furious to trust her voice any further, she bent her head forward and started to type. Very fast and completely innaccurately, and using the ripe sort of language that cheerful secretaries were supposed to know nothing about. She completely forgot that she was using a word processor with a luminous screen and not a good old-fashioned typewriter, until Stefan let out a huge bellow of laughter. Then, head still bent, she pressed the right combination of buttons and wiped her anger off the screen at a stroke. It still seethed inside her, though.

'I'll pick you up at eight,' he called cheerfully as he slammed back into his office.

She had no sooner got home than Gerry appeared. He poured himself a glass of wine from the bottle he

had brought with him, and set about making her laugh.
Ferry raised a couple of synthetic smiles, but that was
all.

'I'm flogging a dead horse tonight, aren't I? What's
the problem, Ferry?'

And so she told him.

'He really said that?' said Gerry, throwing back his
head and laughing. 'What a cretin! You should wear
something really awful . . . something cheap and tasteless
and trashy . . . It would serve him right!'

'It's not funny,' she muttered, biting her lower lip.

'Ferry, it's hilarious! The only response to a comment
like that is to make the man wish he'd never opened his
mouth in the first place . . .'

Ferry sighed. A week ago she might have agreed with
Gerry. A week ago she might have rung Angela and borrowed the jade number with the boned bodice and the
strategically placed tassels. She was stupid. She should
find herself another job tomorrow, instead of waiting
till the end of the fortnight. That was what temping was
supposed to be all about, anyway: freedom.

'No. I'd be letting myself down in my own eyes if I
did that.'

Gerry shrugged irritably. 'Do it your own way. You
always do.' And then he went. Ferry had a dismal feeling
that she might not be seeing so much of Gerry in the
future. Which was a shame. Because he never tried to
kiss her these days. And he could always make her laugh.
Well, usually.

At ten minutes past eight Ferry's doorbell rang. She
looked out through the peep-hole, just in case. It was
Stefan. In a dinner-jacket. Even distorted by the lens he
looked magnificent. She opened the door, stepped
through it and closed it firmly.

'Good lord,' he said condescendingly, 'a woman who's ready on time!'

Ferry smiled a glacial smile. She had been ready on time because she didn't want Stefan coming into her flat and nosing around, making judgements about her based on her possessions. However, there was something in his tone of voice which seemed to suggest that she had been ready on time because she was gauche; over-eager; not a proper laid-back woman of the world. It made her wish she'd been late, after all.

'Good lord,' he said again as he took her elbow to hand her into his Mercedes. The winged eyebrows shot up, furrowing his broad brow. 'That's the real thing, isn't it?'

She glanced down at her soft, dolman-sleeved, wrap around coat. 'Yes,' she agreed. It was silky soft suede, actually, and the most stunning shade of old rose.

'You're full of surprises, aren't you, Ferry?' he said caustically.

'Possibly,' she conceded coolly.

'How on earth do you afford a coat like that on a secretary's salary?'

Hmm. So the lower orders were supposed to know their place, even when it came to coats. 'You'd have preferred me in a plastic mac?' she asked drily.

Stefan chuckled.

Actually the coat had been a gift from her father. Her dear father who had walked out on her mother before Ferry had even been born. A father she had never even met. It had been a shotgun wedding, with Ferry's maternal grandfather metaphorically holding the barrel to the man's head. As soon as Grandpa had grown complacent and put the gun away, the man had bolted. Ferry's mother had always been philosophical about it. 'He wasn't ready for it, Ferry. He still had too much living to do. He was like a caged animal. He would have made us miserable if he'd stayed.' And Ferry had accepted it without question, because she and her mother were happy. Very happy, even though her mother had had to work hard.

They hadn't heard from her father in all those years. Lately, however, having grown older, wiser and, presumably richer, he had started sending Ferry lavish birthday gifts. Ferry accepted them reluctantly. It was a bit late in the day, of course, and typical of a man to think that a few pricy presents could wipe out the past, but he was only trying to do the best he could in the only way he knew how. It would be cruel to throw them back in his face. She refused to meet him, though. She was disturbed to find that she wasn't *that* generous.

When they arrived at the restaurant Ferry shed her coat. She kept a weather eye on Stefan's face, interested in his reaction. She was wearing a discreet Jean Muir in a fine navy silk jersey, exquisitely cut to cling from its high neckline down to her hips, before falling in a swirling rush almost to her ankles, its pleated sleeves gathered at the elbows. The dress had been a Christmas present from her mother, who had also grown richer with the passage of years. Around her neck she wore a short white-gold chain with five diamonds strung along the centre...yet another present from papa. Ferry did well for presents from her parents.

Stefan's reaction amused her. He was watching her coat unwrap and slip from her shoulders, his shoulders relaxed, his eyes alert. Would she be wearing something presentable underneath? After his comments that afternoon she knew he must be apprehensive... His sharp yellow-gold eyes flickered as something modest, discreet, dark and yet dressy made its appearance. They flickered again as she took a few steps and then turned.

The fabric moved like a dream when enticed to mix with air.

He fetched her a spritzer and himself a whisky and soda from the crowded bar. The crowd parted for him. On his way back he took the opportunity to look her up and down once again. He obviously thought that his scrutiny wouldn't be so obvious in the mêlée. Ferry wasn't fooled. Her skin responded to his eyes like a bloodhound to scent, anyway. He was clearly as surprised by his second appraisal as he had been by the first.

He gave her a crooked smile along with her drink. It made her feel cross. She didn't know which would have been worse—for him not to have noticed how good she looked, or the fact that he had done. She was elegant in her muted work clothes too. He had no damned right to look so surprised.

'Come and sit down,' muttered Stefan. 'This is just chit-chat now. A complete waste of time. We won't discuss anything of importance till the brandy arrives. We may as well conserve our energy.'

Ferry followed him mutely to a broad velvet bench, and sat beside him.

'You look terrific,' he said.

She smiled nastily.

He sighed. 'You know you look terrific. Don't you?'

She smiled acidly again.

'What's the matter?'

Ferry looked down at her hands. She linked her fingers neatly in her lap. What was she supposed to say? I wanted you to fancy me from the moment you clapped eyes on me, as I did you? And if he had done? Would she have been able to fall in love with him then? She wasn't in his league. Even in her Jean Muir dress she wasn't in his league. Even without the freckles she wouldn't be.

The whole thing was futile and it was turning her from a cheerful person into a miserable virago. She was ceasing to recognise her limitations and live within them. At any moment she'd fall into the mire of despondency and start wailing and gnashing her teeth.

She flicked her head so that her glossy hair shadowed her face. Get a grip on yourself, you idiot, she told herself sternly. When she looked up she was smiling broadly, the old dry light shining out of her grey eyes.

'I'm sorry, Stefan. I've had a lot on my mind, one way and another. But I'm back in cheerful mode now. Look, why don't you brief me on this crew—I mean, why are we here tonight? What are we hoping to achieve?'

He looked at her very steadily for a moment, then ran his fingers through his hair. 'Bloody cheerfulness,' he said wryly. 'I'd much sooner you were a vegetarian.' Then he began to talk about expanding markets and trade restrictions so fast that he lost her.

CHAPTER FOUR

FERRY tried to keep the cheerful smile stuck firmly in place throughout the meal. She didn't want Stefan thinking that she was miserable. He claimed to want her to drop the façade, but he wouldn't like it if she did. People didn't like you to be glum. She had learned that a long time ago. Oh, she knew Stefan didn't like her, anyway. But she didn't want him to dislike her any more than he already did. She didn't want anyone to dislike her, actually, but for some reason it suddenly seemed imperative that Stefan should stop loathing her so much. So why did she keep saying things to him which just made things worse? And why on earth had she ever allowed herself to try to explain to him why she fought so hard to keep happy?

Resolutely she switched her mind off from that bewildering topic and concentrated instead on chewing a mouthful of steak. It needed chewing, as it happened. It was tough.

'How's your steak, Ferry?' Stefan asked.

'Fine,' she smiled.

He tutted wryly. 'Mendacity, Ferry...' he said softly.

'No,' she murmured insistently, 'not mendacity... manners.'

It brought a small spasm of humour to the borders of his nose. Perhaps he was coming to like her cheerfulness after all? But not sufficiently to keep his head turned her way. Instead he began talking in German to a German taxation expert, making the round, bespectacled face light up with mirth. Before long everyone in

66

their vicinity was giving Stefan their undivided attention. Despite the language barrier she could see that Stefan was charming the socks off them.

Ferry turned to her other neighbour at the table, but the woman was already engaged in conversation. She swallowed a sigh and let her eyes drift around the room. It was a beautiful place. Very modern, very big, with a huge window which looked out across the river. There was a waiter on the far side, sauntering. Oh, dear. No...not a waiter...oh, good gracious, no... Ferry gulped. He was coming in her direction, an insolently complacent grin acting as an indicator to the amount of wine he must have consumed in the few hours since she had seen him last. Oh, lord... How on earth could she have mistaken *Gerry* for a waiter? And it was getting worse by the moment...because he was unbuttoning his shirt and—oh, good grief—he was wearing no shoes— completely barefoot—and... Oh, *no*. He was stripping off all his clothes and dropping them carelessly on the floor as he crossed the enormous room.

The conversation faded as all eyes turned to the spectacle of a tall, lean man, dressed at last in nothing but a leopard-skin loincloth, heading directly for their table.

'Gerry...' she muttered in a strangulated whisper.

Stefan turned his head at the shocked little sound and stared hard into Ferry's frozen face. Her blood was creeping in her veins. Her nerves prickled. She turned, dry-mouthed, towards Stefan. The smile on his face was widening and his nostrils flared as it became increasingly obvious where Gerry was headed. Why was he amused? Didn't he realise that Gerry was about to humiliate him most horribly? Then, when Gerry arrived behind Ferry and laid a hand possessively on her shoulder, Stefan finally baffled her completely by pushing back his chair with an air of relaxed ease and getting to his feet.

'Hey...' he boomed affably. 'The flowers, you goon. You've forgotten the flowers...' And he slapped Gerry on his naked white shoulder and ushered the bewildered chap out of the room with an air of such good-natured *bonhomie* that Ferry was dumbfounded.

The conversation creaked back into life. Ferry was overcome with fear. What was going to happen next? Why had Stefan said that about the flowers and swept Gerry outside? What on earth was going on out there? The diners fell silent as Stefan resumed his seat, beaming roguishly by now, his amber eyes glittering. Behind him padded Gerry, looking a good deal less complacent, and with a basket of red roses in his hands. He gave Ferry a reluctant peck on the cheek, handed her the flowers, glared disconsolately into her eyes, and then turned on his heel and stalked off.

'Bloody kissogram service is going to pieces these days,' Stefan said wryly. 'I expected a bit more than that for my money! Still, hopefully I'll reap my reward later...'

A few of the diners laughed, as if Stefan had said something very funny. But Ferry was too rigid with panic to understand what was going on.

And then something quite extraordinary happened. Stefan's hand came up and touched the back of her neck in the gentlest of caresses. She almost jumped out of her skin at his touch. He must be absolutely seething, and yet his fingers were moving softly against her skin, stroking the fine hairs in the most tender way imaginable. Why on earth was he doing that? She felt her warm face rage even hotter, and, infuriatingly, in the midst of all this dreadful mortification, arousal began to shimmer inside her like a heat-haze. Her skin was alive with it. Her stomach knotted with it. She felt her nipples peaking against the silk jersey. Thank goodness her elbows were masking her breasts. Thank goodness the fabric was dark in colour. The proud points would cast a less obvious shadow...Oh, lord...oh, lord... She had experienced fleeting intimations of her own sexuality when she'd allowed her eyes to linger on Stefan in the office. But it had been a very diluted thing compared to this piquant reality.

The dry pressure of his fingers continued to stir against her neck. She dropped her eyes to her hands folded neatly on the table. What was going on? Somewhere, beyond the sound of the blood roaring in her ears, she could hear good-humoured laughter. It shook out of the crowd at the table. More particularly it rumbled up from the nearness of Stefan's body. And then the hand moved from the back of her neck, and came possessively around her shoulder. He was leaning a little towards her, and drawing her into the crook of his arm as if they were...well, lovers...and he was proud to be cuddling her in public.

She dropped her hands into her lap and risked looking outwards. The boring beaurocrats on the other side of the table were smiling very genially at her. Very indulgently. And when she dared to turn her head and look up at Stefan, very meekly from under her very straight fringe, she found that he was smiling indulgently at her too.

'Was that a dreadful surprise, darling?' he asked roguishly.

'Er—I...'

'I'm sorry. I really didn't mean to embarrass you. I just wanted to let the world know in no uncertain terms that you are mine this evening... I'm afraid you bring out the caveman in me. I get very protective...'

'I...uh...' She steeled herself to look into his eyes. They were glittering with malicious mirth. And not the least bit indulgent.

'Don't say anything, darling,' he murmured softly. 'Just keep gazing into my eyes like that. It's very convincing.' His fingers curled around the top of her arm, and his thumb began to trace sensuous patterns on the skin beneath the fine fabric of the sleeve.

Ferry blinked once, very slowly. Why was he behaving like this, when he must be absolutely raging with fury inside? If only he'd let go of her she could rearrange her brains and try to work it out, but the very proximity of him, the bold weight of his arm across her shoulder, his hand upon her flesh, was having such a powerful effect on her body that coherent thought was out of the question. And then, to make it worse, he brought his face towards hers and let his firm lips brush against her cheek. She felt the barb of his chin against her skin, inhaled his male tang, and then an involuntary shudder ran through her. Oh, hell and damnation. There was no way he could have failed to notice *that*.

'Good gracious, Ferry,' he murmured. 'What on earth induced that delicious little shiver?' He paused, then added sardonically, 'Shame, I should hope...raw, unadulterated shame...'

She arranged a submissive smile on her features. 'What the hell are you up to?' she whispered, taking care not to move her lips.

'Saving my face, sweetheart. What else? Or did you think I was doing all this just for you? You have a little explaining to do, but we'll keep it for later, huh? In the meantime let's just go on letting everyone think that I arranged for Tarzan to come and warn the other males off my *darling* girl...'

'Right...' breathed Ferry, understanding at last. He gave her an affectionate little hug. Well, it wasn't an affectionate little hug at all, really. She could hardly fail to be aware of that. But at least it looked like one and felt like one. She lifted her eyes to the world and smiled in what she hoped was a convincingly love-lorn manner. Oh, lord. That Gerry. He deserved to be hung, drawn and quartered. She'd strangle him with her bare hands if he ever came crawling around to her flat again. This was awful. What on earth was going to happen next?

What happened next was possibly even worse. The brandy arrived, and with it the time for serious talking. Stefan disentangled himself from her in the most sickeningly tender of ways, and turned back to the German taxation expert on his left.

'That new proposal you mentioned earlier sounds quite fascinating,' he began.

'Ha! But not as fascinating as your young lady. That much is clear. And we always think that you British men are so cold fishes...'

She could almost hear Stefan's teeth grinding in his head, but his face pretended amusement. 'Ah, but I'm half Hungarian, you know. The wild, gypsy blood...'

A babble of laughter arose. Stefan had been claiming attention all evening. Now he was paying for it. All heads in the immediate vicinity were turned towards him, everyone eager to tease him for his romantic streak. You had to hand it to the man—he carried it off with remarkable aplomb. Every time he tried to start a serious discussion, someone would turn the conversation back to his flamboyantly romantic gesture, and every time they did that his arm would slide protectively around Ferry's shoulder, while she, in turn, simpered in what she hoped was a suitable manner. If nothing else, the experience proved that all the world loved a lover. Or at least these particular representatives of the EC did.

The whole experience was having the most disastrous effect on Ferry. All this embarrassment should have ensured that she never wanted to clap eyes on the man again. But instead she couldn't keep her eyes off him any more than he was pretending not to be able to keep his hands off her. And all the while her blood sang in her veins, her breasts positively hummed, and deep within her a heady warmth was spreading its tempting fingers. She felt light-headed with desire.

When it became clear that from a business point of view the evening was a complete wash-out, Stefan smiled benignly at the company and murmured something about having an early night. The remark brought a low chuckle from one or two of the diners, and a scalding flush to Ferry's cheeks. His arm went to her elbow, and with gratitude she allowed him to lead her from the table and out of the room into the empty foyer beyond. He had the basket of flowers in the other hand, but handed them discreetly to a waiter, murmuring something about returning them to room 203, with thanks.

'My coat,' she gulped. 'I'll just get my coat. I'm so terribly sorry, I really——'

But she didn't manage to finish the sentence. A few of the diners had drifted out in their wake. Stefan's head came down and his mouth covered hers and he began to kiss her so convincingly that her body was fooled, even though her mind knew exactly what was going on. His mouth opened over hers as though they were the most familiar of lovers. His arms wrapped around her shoulders, his fingers curling delectably against her back. She could feel herself blushing with embarrassment. And then Stefan's tongue began to probe insistently against her lips and suddenly she had to struggle to remember that this was nothing but a ploy... a game... And then, to her horror, her own mouth started to open to him and she let his tongue curl past her teeth, till it arrived, warm and persuasive against her own.

It was a game... to save his face... that was all... but it didn't feel as if that was what it was. Not at all. Her own arms reached around his waist quite automatically—and not because she was afraid someone was looking and she needed to play her part. They insinuated themselves around him because they wanted to. They did it all by themselves. They wanted to do it so badly that nothing in the world was going to stop them. And as her hands felt the packed mass of muscle and bone beneath his clothes her mouth began to respond to the passion of his kiss. Ferry had been kissed by a man before. But this was the very first time she had ever kissed a man in return. She closed her eyes, savouring the taste of him on her tongue, the firm pressure with which his lips worked over hers, the arousing demands of his mouth exploring her mouth, of her mouth exploring his.

When he stopped kissing her the air against her moist skin sent a sudden chill right down to her toes. He kept his arms around her and leaned back to survey her face. This altered his centre of gravity. It meant that he had to thrust his hips forward in order to remain standing. It meant that bone crushed against bone. With a faint gasp she jumped backwards. His nostrils widened, and then quivered.

'What a modest little soul you are, Ferry,' he commented drily. 'It's OK, I'm only checking that they've gone. What did you think I was up to?'

'I should have thought that was obvious,' she sighed, pulling out of his arms.

Stefan laughed drily.

'Can I just get my coat?' she pleaded. 'Look, I'm awfully sorry about everything. But can we just get out of this place before I grovel properly?'

One thick, honey-coloured eyebrow tilted a little. He pressed his lips hard together. 'OK,' he said softly.

Ferry pulled a face. 'Come on, then,' she said, hurrying towards the cloakroom. Her skirt swirled seductively against her legs. She shivered again at the delicacy of the sensation. Oh, stop it, she raged inwardly. Turn yourself off, girl. It's all been a game. Why can't you understand that? But her body didn't turn itself off.

She practically snatched her coat from the attendant, and was dismayed when Stefan came loafing towards her and took it from her, holding it out for her to put on. She slipped her arms into the loose sleeves, her back to him. But before she could wrap it firmly around herself he dropped a hand over her shoulder and let it come to a rest on her right breast. His thumb found the nipple, and teased it. Flinching again, she stepped forward and grasped the edges of the coat fiercely. Then, holding it closed with one arm, she picked up her bag from the table and began walking.

'Hey.' He was beside her, his arm around her shoulder. 'I'm a possessive lover, remember? Take it easy...'

She would have to play along. In the circumstances she had no choice. And Stefan was relishing it.

Just in front of the main entrance he stopped again and caught her close against him. 'They're bringing my car around,' he murmured into her hair. 'Let's play to the camera while we're waiting, huh?'

'There's no camera,' she muttered. 'And no audience. Not out here. Not any more.'

But he ignored her, and ducked his head to claim her mouth again. This time she found herself instantly taking up where they had left off minutes before. She didn't

bide her time before opening her mouth and letting him
plunder it with his kiss. She just couldn't help herself.
It was too tempting. Her normally astute mind blanked
out all the horrors of the past hour. Suddenly she knew
nothing but the pulsing pleasure of sensation. She was
kissing him back with all the passion she felt rippling
though her. Her fingers splayed against his jacket, then,
craving more, they slipped up beneath the fabric to rest
against the shirt beneath. Now she could feel the heat
of his body, sense the very texture of his skin, grasp the
powerful weight of muscle cloaking his massive frame.
She moved closer to him, her round, high breasts
crushing against the tiny pleats of his shirt. His tongue
was rapacious, delving hard within her mouth, his broad
hands mobile as they held her close against him.

She felt him breathe in and out. She felt his flat, hard
stomach advance and retreat against her trembling frame.
She recognised the solidity of his thigh as it brushed
against her own. Her breasts seemed to be bursting
against him, engorged with desire, craving an even closer
contact, an even sweeter response. How she longed to
let her hands travel downwards till they claimed the
proud curve of his buttocks. But she dared not...it would
be *too* wanton...would reveal too clearly how she felt...
Ohh...what on earth was happening to her?

He slid his arms inside her coat, which had fallen open,
and let one hand cup her breast. He fondled it enticingly
beneath the cover of her coat, while his mouth did all
those wonderful things they had done before. Then his
thumb found the eager nipple and began to trace its contours again. It was too much. She dragged her face away
from his and took in a deep breath.

'Stop it,' she pleaded, whisperingly.

But he didn't stop it. He rested his mouth against her
hair and let his own breath warm her scalp. Meantime

his thumb continued to do exactly what it had been doing before, only a little faster, and with a little more pressure.

The urgency of her desire began to mount. 'No...' she wailed, frightened by the alarming sensations he was stirring inside her. But he paid no attention to her protest. This is not happening to me, she told herself, closing her eyes. I don't respond like this to men. I'm frigid. I'm not even capable of falling in love. I wish he'd stop. I think I'm going to melt... I want it to go on forever...

The car arrived. Her legs were shaking so much that she could hardly walk. Once she was safely installed inside the car she fumbled inside her coat with trembling fingers to find the silk ties which held it closed. She knotted them firmly, then folded her arms across her chest.

Stefan looked at her lionishly once he was behind the wheel. His lips pressed together in a cynical smile. He laughed a short, abrupt laugh, then he pulled away into the tangle of headlights and street-lamps beyond. Ferry ran her tongue over her swollen lips. Oh, lord... what would happen now? Anxious to change the mood, she rummaged in her bag and produced her notepad and a pen. 'If you would like to dictate anything I'm quite capable of writing while you drive,' she muttered quaveringly.

He was silent for a moment. 'I've told you before now that I'm not a fool,' he said, his voice unexpectedly hard with irritation.

'I...I realise that you weren't able to have the discussions you hoped for, but just in case there was anything you wanted me to make a note of then I just want you to know that I'm quite willing.'

'I'd already gathered that you are quite willing, Ferry,' he said brusquely, bringing the colour flooding to her cheeks again.

'I'm not, actually. I mean...well, I mean that I was only too glad to pretend, you know, for your sake and everything, because really it was all my fault, but what I mean is I'm not sort of willing otherwise. You know. Anything but, actually.'

'Did you take lessons in speaking English badly?' he snapped.

'No. I mean...what I mean is...you see...' She gave up in despair. She sighed. How on earth did one set about apologising for *everything* when you were sitting on a volcano of unsatisfied lust?

He took in a sharp breath. 'Tell me something, Ferry,' he said sardonically. 'What did you do to the guy?'

'Er—Gerry?'

He gave an incredulous snort. 'Gerry? For crying out loud, Ferry, what in heaven's name induced you to make cow-eyes at a man called Gerry? Gerry and Ferry... Do you have a glittering future as a music hall double-act lined up? Is that what this evening's performance was all about? A rehearsal for something even grander?'

Ferry sighed querulously. 'Of course not,' she muttered, and then added a little more defiantly, 'And at least I know his name, which is more than can be said for you when it comes to your—um—your *lunchtime diversions*. I had no idea he was going to turn up and try to make an exhibition of you.'

'Ah. I suspected from what he said when I got him outside that I was the real target, not you. He said something about your hair which I shan't repeat, but which indicated that he thought I might have an attitude problem as far as your tresses were concerned.'

Ferry felt herself blush a hot scarlet. Oh, dear. 'I'm sorry,' she murmured with unaffected meekness. Oh, lord. What had got in to Gerry this evening?

'Save your pity for lover-boy. There was no more than a pinkish flush around his eye when he brought you the flowers. The colour should be deepening nicely by now.'

Ferry blinked. 'Oh,' she said faintly. Gerry must have been outrageously rude to have earned himself a black eye. Stefan had many failings, but she suspected he did not make a habit of punching people in the face at internationally sponsored banquets. 'I'm sorry,' she said yet again, this time with even more feeling.

'It was self-defence: hit or get hit,' said Stefan coolly. 'I wouldn't have bothered otherwise. But don't expect me to apologise to *you* for landing one on your alcoholic lover.'

'He *isn't* an alcoholic, as it happens. And he's not exactly my... my lover, either.'

'Not exactly? What is that supposed to mean?' he jeered scornfully.

'Um... well, he's just sort of a friend.'

'A friend? Then forgive me if I fail to congratulate you on the company you keep. Nor, come to that, on your tendency to mendacity...'

'It's not a lie. He's isn't a... a lover.'

He gave a disparaging grunt. 'Really? You mean you have perfectly ordinary common-or-garden *friends* who set about embarrassing you like that? Oh, don't try to explain. I can guess exactly what you've done to the guy, anyway, to make him do something like that.'

Oh, the things she would say to Gerry if ever she saw him again! 'I'll make him pay... honestly——'

'My guess is that you've already done that, Ferry,' he said coldly. 'He wouldn't have had the gall to take off his clothes in public with a ribcage like his if you hadn't already made him pay...'

Ferry closed her eyes tight against a sharp stab of tears. Stefan sounded so scornful of her. He really seemed to pity Gerry for whatever it was he imagined she had done to him. And yet surely she hadn't done anything except tell him how rude Stefan had been? She frowned. Stefan couldn't be right, could he? Was it all her fault? Had her lack of response to Gerry's kisses hurt him *that* deeply? And yet what was she supposed to have done about it? Faked pleasure? Worn a T-shirt, proclaiming 'Don't take it personally, but I'm frigid'? And then suddenly she was more confused than ever because she hadn't felt the least bit frigid when Stefan had kissed her. The tears gathered but she blinked them furiously away.

'I'm sorry,' she said weakly again.

This time Stefan positively hissed with annoyance. 'For God's sake stop apologising,' he growled. 'It's not as if you mean it.'

'But I do. I had no idea——'

'Look, I could tell by your reaction back there that you had no part in organising that grim little farrago. You were too embarrassed to be faking it. But the fact that you found it all embarrassing doesn't mean that you're the least bit sorry that it's happened. Not really, Ferry. Not deep down.'

'Oh, doesn't it?' she exclaimed heatedly. 'And why on earth should you think that?'

'Because your so-called good manners are just like chicken wire—invisible unless you view them from the right angle. Then you're easy to make out, and as scratchy as hell. You wrap yourself up in them when it suits you. You aren't really a well-mannered young lady at all, are you? You're a bitch. Once you tuck up in bed with old Gerry tonight you'll probably laugh your head off.'

Ferry glared at him, white-lipped. 'I've already told you that Gerry and I are only friends. Ex-friends as it happens, because I shan't speak to him ever again after tonight. I've only discussed you with Gerry once—and that was this evening when I told him how insulting I found your offer of a dress and hairdo at the *firm's* expense. I'd already made my feelings plain on that subject to you, so it should have come as no surprise. And, contrary to what you believe, I *am* genuinely sorry about it all. I don't expect you to believe it, but it happens to be the truth.'

There was a brief, stony silence and then Stefan said, 'Oh, dear. What a shame. I rather liked the idea of you loosening up and bad-mouthing me behind my back. I'd have preferred it if you had the guts to say it all to my face, of course. But the idea that you really might be as bland as you make out is very dispiriting.'

If Stefan hadn't been driving the car Ferry would have hit him. Instead she made a guttural sound in her throat which expressed a great deal of the violence she felt. 'I think you're extremely arrogant!' she spat out.

He gave a short, appreciative laugh. 'Go on...' he invited tauntingly, but Ferry only bit her lip.

'Surely you left a bit out,' he goaded.

'I left a great deal out,' she said bitterly. 'I discover, to my annoyance, that I am indeed too well mannered to tell you exactly how horrible I think you are.'

'That wasn't what I meant,' he returned crisply. 'You may think that I'm arrogant. But you also think that I'm attractive as well as arrogant, don't you?'

Ferry gasped. 'You have just proved my point,' she said archly. 'I not only *don't* find you attractive, but I cannot imagine how you can have the arrogance to believe that I do.'

He let out an ironic sigh. 'Mendacity...' he said in a voice so low that it was barely audible.

Well, he was right about that, she found herself thinking, and almost let out a rueful laugh which would have given the game away completely. Oh, yes, of course she found him attractive. Unbearably attractive, though she obviously wasn't about to admit it. Except that now she found she didn't have the nerve to deny it either. She suspected that her voice would give her away. She folded her arms and sealed her lips.

He didn't say any more, either. He just kept his big hands on the wheel and his eyes on the road ahead. Every now and then the hard orange glare of a street-light would flash in through the windscreen, burnishing the hairs on the back of his hands to a flaming bronze. His eyebrows, too, took the colour, making him seem almost diabolical for brief seconds. Ferry wanted to weep. He had never looked more attractive, nor more unattainable. Well, he didn't think she was a nobody any more. Far from it. She realised how lucky she had been to rate so high in his estimation.

When they got to her door she jumped out of the car with astonishing speed.

'Hey... wait...' he called.

'Er—thanks for the lift. Goodnight.' She smiled as cheerfully as she could manage.

But he too had got out of the car and in a few strides was at her side. 'Not so fast,' he said warningly. 'I'm coming in with you.'

Ferry shot him a shocked glance. 'No!' she exclaimed. 'I... It's all right. I can see myself in.'

Stefan shook his head scornfully. 'I intend to escort you safely indoors. I would do the same for any woman.'

'Oh...' Ferry gave him a guarded look as she unlocked the front door.

'There,' she said firmly as she entered the hallway.

But he came in beside her. 'Right into your flat. Safe and sound. That's the way I do it.' His voice was coldly insistent.

Reluctantly she opened the door to her ground-floor flat and stepped inside, snapping on the light. 'Look,' she said, sweeping out an arm to indicate the comfortable room. 'Safe and sound. No evidence of burglars. Nothing.'

Stefan gave her a slow, rather glacial smile. 'Do you live here on your own?' he asked.

Ferry huffed out a huge sigh. 'Yes.'

'Very nice... very nice indeed,' he drawled, and then turned his back on her and left.

CHAPTER FIVE

'WHAT the hell are you doing here?' Stefan stuck his head around the door of her office at eight-ten on Monday morning and glared at Ferry as if her presence appalled him beyond belief.

'I'm usually in at eight. I thought we'd established that.'

'God-damn it, Ferry, I know that. But I expected you to be off in search of some cheapskate travel agency, not creeping back here with your tail between your legs. What are you, some sort of glutton for punishment?'

'Obviously. Though I don't have a tail, and if I did it wouldn't be between my legs. I wasn't responsible for Friday's fiasco, and I take my work too seriously to fail to turn up.'

'Oh, yes. I remember now. We had this conversation last Monday, too. Well, at the risk of repeating myself, let me point out that you are free to leave just whenever you want to. I certainly shan't raise any objections.'

Ferry examined his fierce scowl as calmly as she was able. She wasn't going to let him force her to go scurrying off as if she had done something wrong. 'Is there anything you'd like me to do?' she asked haughtily.

'You can wipe that frosty look off your face, for a start. I can't possibly put up with another week if you walk around looking like that.'

'Sorry, but that's out of the question.'

Stefan gave her a vitriolic glare, then retreated into his room, slamming the door. He buzzed the intercom. 'Coffee?'

Ferry kicked the door aggressively on her way through to fetch coffee and let it slam behind her. Her knees were shaking. She'd spent the entire weekend listing all the reasons why she wasn't going to go back to work for Stefan Redwell. Being a temp had its advantages. One of them was the freedom to walk away from difficult bosses. And yet she had known all along in the back of her mind that Monday morning would find her scurrying for the bus. She wasn't sure why.

She was quite certain about two things however. One was that she no longer had any desire whatsoever to fall in love with the man. And the second was that she now absolutely loathed and detested him. Since Friday night she hadn't felt cheerful once. She had felt miserable and angry. She had tried to console herself with the knowledge that at least she wasn't frigid: that when the right man came along she would be able to respond as readily as she had to Stefan. But it proved no consolation at all because with an agonising prescience she had recognised that there never was going to be a right man now. Bloody Stefan Redwell, with his big bones and crooked nose and amber eyes, had somehow spoiled her for anyone else.

When she took the coffee in to him, blowing furiously on its surface as she went, he was standing by the open window, inhaling traffic fumes and smiling.

'Spring!' he said.

She set the coffee down on his desk. 'I may have been out of line on Friday, but I hardly think that's sufficient reason for you to order me to jump,' she muttered sarcastically.

His nostrils quivered, and then, quite unexpectedly, he spun around and caught hold of her shoulders and began to kiss her.

Ferry had never been so astonished in all her life. On Friday night he had done it because it had been an expedient solution to a problem. At eight twenty-three on a Monday morning he had to be doing it because...well—her heart began to rise—because he wanted to. Surely?

She was too taken aback to protest immediately. And by the time she had gathered her wits sufficiently to resist, his mouth was already crushing hard against hers with the same demanding pressure that had so aroused her the last time. And indeed, the effect this time was not dissimilar—except that her pleasure was enhanced by the knowledge that he was doing this of his own free will. She felt the tip of his tongue dashing against her mouth.

Oh, dear... this was awful... He was a swine and she hated him but the way his tongue was probing against her lips was so delicious, and his smell—salty, male, clean—was unbearably evocative. She put her hands to his upper arms to wrestle him away, but the sensation of his iron muscles beneath the cool, crisp cotton of his shirt simply acted as an invitation to her senses. She made an involuntary moaning noise in the back of her throat. Stop it, her mind protested feebly. But even as she thought it she felt her lips parting to welcome his tongue. Her inner voice began to ask her whether she had no self-respect, but the inner voice drawled out the question lethargically, as if it didn't really care what the answer might be. He was holding her so close to him... She was kissing him back, her eyes closed, her body lapping up the dreamy sensation of being held by him and kissed by him because... because he *wanted* to...

She felt herself lean into him; felt her breasts crush against the breadth of his chest. And then, abruptly, she felt him pull away from her and opened her eyes to catch him looking down on her. He was smiling very broadly.

She looked guardedly up into his eyes, backing off. They were flecked with gold in the morning sun, and punishingly hard and challenging.

'Why on earth did you do that?' she asked nervously.

He shrugged coolly. 'Just testing, Ferry. Just testing my little theory...'

Ferry's hand came up so swiftly that it wasn't until she heard the crack of her palm against his face that she realised what she had done. There was a timeless, frozen moment before her hand started to sting. Which happened at just exactly the same instant that Stefan began to laugh. He let go of her then and rubbed at his cheek, still chuckling.

Ferry's eyes narrowed and her mouth formed itself into a thin, straight line. 'I don't know what you find so funny about it,' she said, almost choking with anger.

But Stefan only shrugged, his eyes still alive with mirth. He sat on the edge of his desk, picked up his Mason's Ironstone cup and began to sip.

White with fury, Ferry turned and swept out of the room, letting the door bang resoundingly behind her. Fortunately she made it as far as the cloakroom before she burst into tears. She shut herself into a cubicle and sat hunched on the seat, soaking the handfuls of loo paper which she grabbed to press against her burning eyes. Every now and then she would try blowing her nose resolutely and forcing the tears into abeyance, but it didn't work. She needed to cry until she was all cried out.

She cried a little for her own humiliation. Mostly she cried for her recklessness in having embarked upon the foolish escapade of trying to make herself feel something for him. For being tempted to turn a mere physical attraction into something more. And a part of her cried with relief that she was crying. At least she was churning inside with humiliation and anger and all sorts of other deep and unfathomable emotions. At least her heart hadn't quite turned to stone yet. There had to be hope… Oh, dear. Even this shaming pain must be better than a vacuum.

Her mother had never cried, in all those long years. Nor had she bothered with men after her all-too-brief marriage. Instead she had studied law, at first by correspondence course, and then at night school, until finally she had qualified as a solicitor. Law had consumed her. It had become her passion. Contract law. Very dusty; very dry; very obscure. All the time that Ferry had been growing up there had been a space in her mother's heart for her daughter. They had been happy. But once Ferry had got her first job her mother had been free to love law utterly. Ferry's mother wasn't empty inside. She was solidly packed with carefully chewed and digested clauses and statutes and precedents. She had become a senior partner with a top London firm. She was obsessed by her work. She resented bank holidays and went to the office even when she had the flu. She got her secretary to send Ferry designer dresses for her birthdays. Sometimes she rang Ferry up for a chat or called down to the flat she had had converted for Ferry's seventeenth-birthday present, when Ferry had proved reluctant to leave home. She still cared for Ferry, obviously. But Ferry knew that the space which had once belonged to her exclusively was stacked with facts these days. She was no longer the party of the first party as far as her mother was concerned.

Ferry had never wanted to be like her mother. She had wanted there to be space inside her for friendships; for the small pleasures that life could offer; for emotion. And it was a huge relief, she had to admit, as she wept yet more tears into her sodden handful of perforated

tissue, to know that the spaces were all capable of being
filled. But oh, dear, it did hurt to have been used like
that by Stefan. And oh, it was such a bitter humiliation
to have been so palpably moved by a kiss that was to
him no more than a taunt. Please, she willed as she
sniffed her final sniff and emerged from the cubicle to
wash her face, oh, please let him do something pompous
soon. Let me be able to walk out of this mess.

When she got back to her office, her freckles thank-
fully masking the blotchiness of her skin, she opened
her window to let in some fresh air. Then she sat gloomily
at her desk and began investigating the contents of her
in-tray.

She heard doors banging somewhere, but paid no attention to them. Tracey on Reception would let her know
if he went out of the building, anyway. It was nice having
the window open. The sounds wafting in were the sounds
of real, ordinary life. The sort of life she wanted to get
back to. She could even hear Stefan's door bang in stereo
since she had opened the window. The noise came to
her muffled from the gallery—and at the same time
crisper, floating out through his open window and in
through her own. She could hear the voices, too...

'It's no good, Stefan... If you won't marry me then
I think it would be better if I found myself another job.'

'Absurd. It's all been going famously. You're over-
reacting.'

'I'm not.'

'You are. Why does marriage have to be the only
option? It's ridiculous. Everything's been going
swimmingly.'

'But you don't trust me. If you did you'd marry me.'

'Rosa! Of course I trust you. Don't I give you enough?
Is that the problem? Look... I'll write you a cheque.
Name the amount. Will that convince you...?'

There was a momentary hesitation, and when she spoke again she sounded less certain. 'Stefan, I don't actually want more money—or, at least, I do, but that's not the point. I want to put everything on a more secure footing. Oh, we've been through it all time and again! Why do you have to be so perverse?'

'I'm not perverse. You know my reasons.'

'Huh! I know what you claim to believe. But I think you're fooling yourself—and me. You say that we just need a little more time, but I think you just don't want to give your mother the satisfaction——'

'Rosa!'

'You can consider my resignation effective as of now. If you won't marry me then I certainly shan't go on working for you. It would be impossible.'

'For God's sake! What's the matter with you, Rosa? After all these months, and with everything we've got going for us... Everything's been going so superbly well... and yet just because I won't fall in with your ideas here and now you want to ruin it all.'

Ferry could almost *hear* them glaring at each other.

'Goodbye, Stefan.'

There was a banging door. Then a long silence. And then a heated expletive followed by a furiously muttered, 'Oh, damn it. She's cut off her silly little nose to spite her face now. Well, it serves her right, but it's bloody inconvenient all the same...'

Ferry sat very quietly at her desk, round-eyed with astonishment. A curious mixture of emotions had been stirred by the overheard exchange. She was horrified at the cold-bloodedness of it all. There had been about as much heartfelt emotion in it as there was in the average cheese and onion roll. Less. At least the onions would be capable of producing a few crocodile tears. That pair had sounded more *irritated* with each other than any-

thing. Oh, well, if that was how Stefan Redwell conducted his affairs, it was a good job she was so safe from
his attentions.

And yet, ironically, she found exhilaration stirring
inside her, too. At least she knew for certain that Stefan
was heart-free now. There was Clementine and Belinda,
of course, but he could never remember their names. If
nothing else she could be confident that it hadn't exactly
been love at first sight with either of them...

Slowly she leaned forward and banged her forehead
on her desk. She hated men. What on earth was she
doing letting her thoughts run on like that?

Naturally he chose that moment to walk in. 'Collapsed through overwork, Ferry?' he jeered.

'Yoga,' she said, keeping her forehead where it was.
Anything had to be better than looking at him.

'I would have thought you could find more interesting
ways to relax than that,' he growled.

She straightened up and met his eye. 'Well, I've tried
kissing the boss already this morning. It wasn't very effective. My heart wasn't in it.'

'You mean you'd let a little thing like that stop you?
Well, you do surprise me...'

She blinked very slowly and very disdainfully. 'If I
took two hours for lunch every day I might manage
something more stimulating by way of a hobby,' she said.
'But as it is I make do with a little yoga at my desk...'

'Ah, yes. That little plan of yours for keeping happy...
What was it? Accept that there are limits and get what
you can out of them?'

He sounded so deprecating that she felt anger lurch
inside her like a flat-bottomed boat on a choppy sea.
She must have been mad to try to explain herself to him.

'Quite,' she responded stiffly, watching his back disappear through the door. He clearly wasn't about to let her distract him with her crackpot theories *this* morning.

He was in a filthy mood for the rest of the day. Matters weren't helped by the fact that a crisis blew up about an order which had gone astray in Saudi Arabia. The distribution manager was, luckily, in Birmingham. Ferry had a suspicion he would have found himself looking for a new job if he'd been on hand. And Stefan apparently was so unbelievably rude to the receptionist when he stormed out for his protracted lunch-hour in the Bacchinalean that the poor girl put in her notice. He must have been more upset about Rosa than he'd appeared.

Ray sidled into her room, eager to gossip. 'Two in one day,' he said with a conspiratorial wink. 'Miss Barton's gone as well, you know? Goodness knows what's going on. Mind you, she'd been in love with him for months, so I'm not surprised. It doesn't do to have that kind of thing going on in the workplace, does it? Especially in this day and age. Women like to be taken seriously when it comes to their work, don't they? But you can't expect a man like him to take a woman seriously if she's soft on him. It wouldn't make sense, would it? Anyway, the reason I'm telling you is, you could be in with a chance, see, being on the spot. I'd go up to Personnel if I were you and ask for a form. At least *you're* not the silly sort of type who goes falling in love with her boss...'

Ferry smiled grimly. 'Thanks, Ray,' she murmured, surprised by his newly liberated viewpoint. Stefan must have had a word with him after all. Oh, well. At least she'd had a positive impact on Ray's life, even if her own was falling to bits.

The next day Stefan was every bit as foul-tempered. He came banging into her office, slapped a list of names on her desk and asked her to track down the relevant files. 'We've sold stuff to all these girls' families at some time or another,' he muttered. 'Get hold of them and fix them up for lunch with me.'

'Together or separately?' Ferry asked primly.

He gave her such a cold look that her blood halted its progress through her circulatory system.

'Separately. Lunches at the Bacchinalean, I think. I'm looking for a replacement for Rosa. A first-class girl with the right sort of background. A *really* good secretary...'

'Aren't I——?' Ferry nearly bit off her tongue. She didn't even want to be offered the job! It was just that she was so used to being praised for her work, so used to being offered permanent positions, that she was shocked rigid when the familiar plaudits failed to arrive. She ran her tongue over her lips. 'Ah...the Bacchinalean...yes...' she said feebly, trying to cover up for her runaway tongue.

'No,' he said, propping his buttocks on the edge of her desk and folding his arms. He surveyed her critically over his high, wide cheekbones. 'No, Ferry. You are not a really good secretary. You are too supercilious and bland to be a really good secretary. I thought that was understood?'

Ferry swallowed her annoyance and looked away. 'Shall I begin the interviewing process by asking these girls whether they have a tendency to be either supercilious, bland or cheerful, when I speak to them, sir?' she asked.

'Don't call me sir. I've told you that before.'

She turned her gaze back on him. 'I can't think what came over me,' she snapped. 'After all, the title usually implies at least a modicum of respect. I doubt it will happen again.'

He tilted his head and ran his fingers impatiently through his hair. 'That's better,' he said coldly. 'Much,

much better. Keep sharpening your tongue like that and you might end up halfway human by the time you draw your pension. But it'll be too late for my purposes, Ferry. I need a really good secretary by Monday.'

'I'll see what I can do...'

Later in the morning he came through again. He was wearing a blue shirt and the trousers of today's charcoal suit with a pair of red braces purporting to keep them in place. Ferry got out of her seat and opened the top drawer of the filing cabinet. The braces had to be superfluous. There was no way those trousers could accidentally slide down over such a muscular pair of hips. They would need to be tugged... Ferry bit her lip and bowed her head over the drawer. She was very tempted to scream. *Anything* to blot out the stupid thoughts which filled her mind every time she found herself in the same room as him.

'Was there something you wanted?' she asked.

'I wanted to tell you that I've checked with Personnel. Mark's secretaries have lasted on average nine weeks. And they've all been under twenty-two.'

She looked over her shoulder at him. 'I see.'

He groaned. 'Back to being bland, Ferry?'

She met his eye, then flinched and looked away. He was too damned attractive by half. When his eyes took on that lazy, satisfied look her bones practically melted. 'Are you going to do anything about Mark?' she asked briskly.

'I've found him a new secretary. She's fifty-seven. And I've also had a little word with Ray.'

Ha! She'd known it! 'Uh-huh,' she murmured noncommittally.

'Stop gloating, Ferry.'

She gave him a defiant glare. 'Am I gloating? I wasn't aware of it...'

'Liar. You love being right, don't you?'

Ferry kept glaring. But inside she didn't feel anywhere near as defiant as she looked. No, she thought. I don't like being right. I don't like being right about my inability to fall in love, for instance. I don't like being so damned right about everybody and everything. I'd rather be wrong, as it happens.

'Don't *you*?' she challenged.

'Not always,' he said, narrowing his eyes. Then he added, 'I knew I could stop you being so bloody cheerful, for instance. I was right about that. However, what I hadn't anticipated was how unpleasant the alternative was going to be.'

'Serves you right,' she said bitterly, poking her nose back into the filing cabinet.

He let out one of his great gusts of laughter. 'It does rather, doesn't it?' he said. 'I shall have to think up another plan to get things going my way.'

When he had gone she slumped into her chair. She had been right about her cheerful demeanour. It had actually contributed to her happiness in all sorts of ways. It made people like her, for a start, and reminded her to keep her mood in tune with her features. But now the smile, like the emotion it proclaimed, eluded her. She had started out wanting so much happiness from life. Now she didn't even have the smile.

It had all started that day with the tinsel. Her mother had shaken her head at the old, familiar paper chains which had served them in the little, shabby house they had rented while her mother had studied. Now that she'd bought this big house the old decorations just wouldn't do.

'That's better,' her mother had said, opening the box full of smart new trimmings. But Ferry hadn't thought that they were better at all. Her eyes had smarted as she'd taken the dusty old paper lanterns out to the bin. She had tucked one inside her jumper and smuggled it up to her newly decorated bedroom. She knew her mother wouldn't approve. 'Forward, Ferraleth,' her mother used to say. 'Go forward. Never look back with regrets.'

Well, they had moved forward. Her mother's hard-won career was flourishing. They had moved into this big house, and suddenly her eternally happy mother was dissatisfied and worried about what other people would think. Ferry looked back with longing. Her mother had less and less time for her, and, no matter how hard she tried to please, her mother seemed to be growing less and less fond of her. She would hate it if she found out about the paper lantern. And more than anything the adolescent Ferry had wanted her mother's approbation. She had looked at herself in the bedroom mirror. She had wiped her eyes with the back of her hand and smiled, but the smile hadn't been at all convincing. She had adjusted the corners of her mouth upwards. She had screwed up her eyes to conceal the fact that in their grey depths there was no trace of happiness. Squinting into the mirror she had carefully fine-tuned her features until she'd achieved the desired effect. Satisfied at last, she'd kept the smile in place till she got back to the sitting-room.

'You're looking cheerful, Ferry,' her mother had said.

'Yes,' Ferry had replied brightly. 'Yes. I'm always cheerful.'

And her mother had smiled a bright smile of her own in return. 'Good...' she had said. 'That makes two of us.'

What had gone wrong? Ferry *had* been happy. She had learned that her mother's obsession with her career had not meant that she hadn't cared and they had settled into a comfortable, mature relationship with each other. She had chosen a lifestyle which left doors open all over the place. She had marched cheerfully into adulthood, waiting for life to get better and better and better, excitedly waiting to peek through all those doors.

The doors were all still open. She'd had lots of interesting jobs in lots of interesting places. And lots of friends, both male and female, and lots of holidays and lots of sun. It was just that Ferry no longer had the desire to walk through those doors. She was too terribly afraid that there would be nothing waiting for her on the far side.

On Wednesday, when she got back from lunch, he was sitting in her chair, his legs stretched out, balancing the heel of one foot on the toe of the other, with his hands folded behind his head. He took a deep breath, so that the cotton of his shirt tautened briefly. He was clearly waiting for her, his eyes half closed, watching the door.

'You like holidays, Ferry, don't you?' he asked as soon as she had crossed the threshold.

'Yes,' she said, hanging up her mac.

'So your passport's up to date?'

'Yes.'

'Good. Ring Gerry and tell him you won't be seeing him for a few days, there's a good girl.'

Ferry looked down at him. He was still breathing. What a shame. Underneath that spasmodically tightening shirt beat his cold, cold heart. 'I've already told you that I shan't be seeing Gerry again. You've chosen to think me a liar from the start. You're wrong.'

He looked up at her insolently. 'I'm not. You're a fraud, Ferry. Even this frosty act you're putting on is a fake. OK, so I believe now that you aren't seeing your music-hall comic any more. But the trouble with liars is

FREE BOOKS CERTIFICATE

Yes! Please send me **Four FREE Temptations** together with my **FREE gifts.**
Please also reserve a Reader Service subscription for me. If I decide to subscribe, I shall receive four superb new titles for just £7.80 each month postage and packing FREE. If I decide not to subscribe, I shall contact you within 10 days. Any free books and gifts will remain mine to keep. I understand that I am under no obligation whatsoever - I may cancel or suspend my subscription at any time simply by contacting you. I am over 18 years of age.

7A4T

Ms/Mrs/Miss/Mr _____

Address _____

_____

_____

Postcode _____

Signature _____

A FREE GIFT

Return this card and we'll also send you this cuddly Teddy Bear absolutely FREE.

A FREE GIFT

We all love mysteries, so AS WELL as your FREE books and Teddy Bear we've an intriguing gift for you.

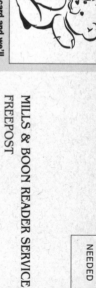

MILLS & BOON READER SERVICE
FREEPOST
PO BOX 236
CROYDON
CR9 9EL

NO
STAMP
NEEDED

that they're rarely consistent. One doesn't know what to believe.'

She shrugged. 'That's your problem, not mine. Now what's all this stuff about passports?'

He tilted his head to one side. 'Business, Ferry. Regretfully I need you with me on a business trip. To Hungary. We'll fly out today.'

She studied him carefully. One big hand unlocked itself from the other and ran itself through his hair, pushing it hard back from his forehead.

'What are you playing at, Stefan? You can't possibly need to take me anywhere,' she said fiercely. 'Just testing your little theory a bit further, eh?'

His jaw tucked marginally closer to his neck in a gesture of agreement. But instead of admitting that she was right he merely said, 'Theory? This is business, Ferry. We've got a big problem over there. I need to go and sort it out. And I need a secretary with me.'

'How can you have a big problem when all you do is move knives and forks from A to B? You lost a gold candelabra worth a quarter of a million in Saudi Arabia the other day. You didn't need to whisk me off to Riyadh to sort that one out.'

He lifted his shoulders contemptuously. 'This is more important. It's connected with that file I asked you to look at last week. I don't have time to brief any one else on the subject, and anyway, you're the only secretary I've got right now.'

'You've got Candice Legrice. She could get here from Sheffield in a couple of hours.'

He looked at her very disdainfully. 'Candice is a *really* good secretary, Ferry. I need her to stay where she is. You, however, are entirely dispensable.'

Ferry's jaw muscles tightened. 'I speak one language,

Stefan. English. My French barely passes muster. So *why* do you need me?'

He shrugged coolly. 'I speak Hungarian. If I needed a translator I'd get a translator. So get a move on and shut up shop here.' His lithe frame tautened as he got to his feet. 'I'll take you home in, say, half an hour and you can pack a few things.'

When he stumped back into his office Ferry asked herself bitterly why on earth she was letting him get away with a stunt like this. He was out to destroy her—to seduce her, probably, even though he didn't really want her at all. Well, just let him try. She'd learned a lot from that one kiss. She didn't like being humiliated, and she was damned if she'd let him get away with it again. She'd go with him to Hungary, though, and she suddenly knew exactly why she'd agreed to the trip. Ferry had one foot in the mire of despondency, and the mire was sucking hard. She couldn't get out. Stefan had pushed her in, and he was the only one who could rescue her, although he'd be astonished if he knew just how she expected him to become her saviour.

The thing was, he'd surely be pompous in Hungary. He'd flaunt his fluency in the language, for a start. Perhaps he'd patronise the people they were going there to see. And he'd show her the blue Danube as if he, personally, were responsible for its very existence. She'd been away on business trips before. She knew what a boss was like, alone in hotels, far from home, with a tall, slim, elegantly dressed secretary with shining hair at his side. Freckled or not. Stefan couldn't be *that* different. Surely?

CHAPTER SIX

ON THE way to her flat Stefan said expansively, 'We'll stop off and get you some nice matching luggage.'

Ferry almost choked on her anger. So the world's drabest woman needed to be supplied with a large and visible status symbol if she was to be seen at an international airport with the King of the Beasts, huh? Good. He was bordering on the pompous already.

'I have luggage, Stefan, thank you,' she returned in what used to be her sweet voice, but which had inexplicably turned to bitter, burnt caramel in her throat.

He shrugged. 'Have it your own way. But I would have paid.'

He sat in the car while she packed. Her own luggage, actually, was lightweight nylon, serviceable and shabby. She dithered for a moment. Oh, drat him... Why should she let him get away with it? She ran upstairs and borrowed a couple of gloriously squidgy blue leather holdalls. Her mother wouldn't mind. She took a ready-made meal out of the freezer while she was up there, and put it on top of the microwave to defrost. Her mother never remembered to eat properly.

Stefan refused to let *her* sit in the car while he packed, though. She was forced to accompany him up the ringing iron staircase to the balcony which opened on to his Chelsea mews flat. The staircase was ornate, made more so by being decorated with hanging baskets of early flowers. He tried to take her by the elbow as they mounted the steps, but she shook him off.

'They can be slippery,' he said.

'So why don't you get rubber treads for them? It'd make them less noisy as well. And some door springs for the office, while you're at it...'

'What? And destroy an early-warning system that it's taken me years to perfect?' he countered.

She humphed. So that was it... Bang, bang and he was forewarned of the inopportune arrival of the Belindas and Clementines of this world when he was busy playing house with Rosa—or whoever her replacement was going to be.

'I'll wait here,' she said, looking down on the old cobbled stable-yard below. Four or five very expensive cars were parked at one end. The rest of it was bordered with stone tubs of rampant greenery. There were so many narcissi in bloom that the scent was almost cloying.

'Come in,' he said curtly, as if he hadn't heard her, and she did, because there seemed to be no point in arguing. Once in the sitting-room which ran the entire depth of the building, giving views on to the river from the far side, she perched on the edge of a chesterfield. It was possibly the biggest couch she had ever encountered, but was none the less dwarfed by the airy spaciousness of the room. The whole place was both orderly and comfortably untidy, filled with well-worn antiques of, she suspected, considerable value. He treated them as if they had come ready to assemble from the nearest DIY warehouse, flinging his jacket hard at a genuine Queen Anne chair whose wings seemed like little outstretched arms, just waiting to catch whatever he threw at it.

She looked around surreptitiously until she realised that he was watching her.

'Is it what you expected, Ferry?' he asked sardonically.

She pursed her lips. 'I didn't expect anything in particular,' she said archly.

He didn't believe her. 'Come, come...you thought I'd live somewhere much bigger than this, didn't you?'

She had, actually. 'Somewhere big enough to house your extensive range of tableware?' she sniped.

He gave a good-humoured laugh in reply, then set about his packing.

'Damn,' he muttered as he rummaged in a walnut bureau, scattering papers all over the place.

'What you need, Stefan,' she said slyly, 'is a really good secretary...'

He looked up and raised one of his honey-coloured eyebrows. But he didn't bother to reply.

He found the papers he was looking for, and stuffed them into a very ancient briefcase.

Then he crossed the room and opened a door with a nudge of his shoulder. It was his bedroom. He busied himself garnering an assortment of clothes while she looked on. Through the door she could see a colonial-style bed, capable of sleeping not just Stefan, but Rosa, Belinda and Clementine—all at the same time. It was unmade, a beautiful patchwork quilt thrown carelessly over the foot, and the sheets sufficiently rumpled to suggest recent, extensive use. Then he made for the bathroom, which also led directly off the sitting-room. This time his packing took place to the accompaniment of a lot of muttered curses, and a few well-aimed kicks at the fluffy pink mules which lay discarded on the marble floor. A floaty chiffon *peignoir* in a paler pink refused to be kicked, however, and tangled itself around his foot. Ferry had to suck on her cheeks to stop herself laughing. Or crying. Or something.

'Bloody women...' he scowled, rolling the garment into a ball and tossing in into the bath.

When he came back into the sitting room, with a single pig-skin suitcase in his hand, he frowned at her and said,

'So what's the big joke? You've got the most sickly smile I've ever seen in my life plastered right across your face.'

Ferry was taken aback. It was supposed to be her bright, cheerful, ready-for-anything smile, worn to disguise the fact that she had found the evidence of female occupation unbearably dispiriting. Though she couldn't imagine why she should care. Whoever-it-was was a hundred per cent welcome to him, after all. 'Have I?' she asked lamely.

He pulled a face. 'Let's move. We've got to eat before we get on that damned plane.'

'What time is the flight?'

He waggled his head from side to side as if making up his mind. 'There's one in two hours. But I guess we'd better forget that. The next one is sevenish.'

Ferry glanced at her watch. 'Two hours is plenty, surely. We should be able to make it to Heathrow in time.'

He heaved a weary sigh. 'I'll buy you a meal first.'

Ferry frowned. 'I've only recently had lunch.'

He narrowed his eyes and stared at her very rudely. 'What's that got to do with anything?'

'I would have thought that was obvious. It seems dumb to miss the flight just for a meal, especially when I'm not hungry. Couldn't you grab a sandwich at the airport? There'll be food on the plane, anyway.'

He gave a puzzled grimace, as if she had just recited the alphabet backwards in Latin, but didn't say anything more on the subject.

He spent most of his time at the airport on the phone— no doubt explaining to the woman in pink why he wouldn't be available to unpeel her that evening. Ferry had brought her fat bestseller and sat grumpily in the departure lounge trying to concentrate.

When they were settled in their first-class seats Stefan tossed a package on to her lap. It was a large bottle of frighteningly expensive perfume from the duty-free shop.

'What's this?' she complained.

'It was the largest they had,' he returned curtly and closed his eyes.

'But I don't want it,' she persisted, baffled.

'Tough,' he muttered, and pretended to doze.

Ferry sighed crossly and stuck it in her bag. She debated whether or not to ask him about this crisis in Hungary, but decided against it. If he wanted her to know, he'd tell her, and anyway, she couldn't imagine that there really was a crisis which required her presence. Stefan was up to something. Presumably a further exercise in destroying her self-esteem. No doubt he would only consider that their brief working relationship had been a glorious success if the fortnight ended with her in urgent need of psychiatric help. He'd succeeded in getting rid of her smile, but she was damned if she'd let him drag her even further into the mire of despondency.

It was dark when they arrived in Budapest. A limousine was waiting to take them to their hotel, which was some miles out of the city centre on the Buda side, built on top of a hill, and unbelievably sumptuous.

Her rooms, she discovered to her relief, while on the same corridor as his, were not adjoining. She couldn't be sure, but she was fairly certain that part of his scheme would involve testing his Newtonian theory of attraction again—the one which stated that larger bodies invariably attracted smaller ones, especially if the larger one was gilded with hairs and had the most enticing amber eyes, and the smaller one was speckled from top to toe. 'Just let him try...' she muttered under her breath.

He leaned against the door-jamb while the porter set down her soft leather bags, and watched her almost

gloatingly while she peeped into the fabulous bathroom
and enormous bedroom which led off her sitting-room.
Then she crossed to the French doors which gave on to
a balcony, and looked down on the lights of the city.

'I'll take you down town for an authentic goulash
later,' he said.

She glanced at her watch. It was nearly nine. 'Isn't it
a bit late?' she frowned.

'No stamina, Ferry?' he queried.

'It depends on what it's required for,' she returned
warningly.

His eyes betrayed his amusement. 'We'll find out,
won't we? Meantime, settle in—— Oh, and Ferry—get
me this number. I'll be in my room.'

The phone number had a Sheffield code. Fortunately
the switchboard operator spoke excellent English, but
Ferry couldn't help being annoyed. OK, so she was os-
tensibly here to work—though if she believed *that* she'd
be believing there were fairies at the bottom of the garden
next. Stefan was probably ringing his mother for form's
sake or something. He was just trying to make this seem
like a bona fide business trip, but she wasn't fooled. He
treated work with a casualness which almost amounted
to indifference—and which, judging by his share prices,
he could clearly afford to do. Redwell's was astonishingly profitable. He had enough natural ability in his
little finger to make running a diverse company like
Redwell's no more than a minor distraction. He was an
archetypal playboy, complacently pursuing his hedon-
istic lifestyle, using his client-list as a kind of dating
agency, and with a family firm to provide entertainment
for his business brain when his social life failed to satisfy.

Ferry didn't approve. She soaked in her sumptuous
bath and enumerated all the ways in which she didn't
approve of this boss of hers. She couldn't find one aspect

of his character and lifestyle of which she did approve. So how come, she thought, slapping the palm of her hand hard against the surface of the bath-water, and sending foam flying into the air like snow, how come she was letting him undermine her like this? She felt perpetually charged with anger; she felt threatened and intimidated by him, no matter how hard she struggled to conceal it; and she felt deep-down unhappy at the sickening realisation that she couldn't stop herself being attracted to him. She clenched her teeth and hissed. If she didn't watch out he was going to succeed in destroying her peace of mind completely.

She dressed in a simple jacket and skirt in pale grey silk, with a gun-metal silk camisole underneath. Then she sat on her sofa and alternately read her book and gazed out over the city. She had to admit to being excited by the visit. She loved travelling—though usually she was forced to stick to cut-price package holidays in predictable locations for reasons of economy. Travel always heightened her sense of doors being open—of life waiting. Her last couple of jaunts had lacked that edge, presumably because they had been high-season visits to busy resorts. But this trip had stirred up all the old excitement.

Stefan didn't reappear until well after ten.

'Ready?' he said. He looked preoccupied.

'I am. But I'm a bit concerned about the time. I thought we had important business to attend to in the morning.'

He eyed her lazily. 'Don't we have important business to attend to tonight as well?' he asked, and his face suddenly broke into one of its lionish smiles.

Ferry suppressed the shiver of awareness which ran through her and eyed him suspiciously. 'You mean that you have a target to reach on demoralising me? You're behind time and want to catch up?'

'Demoralising you?' he repeated slowly. 'You mean you actually have morals, Ferry?'

She swallowed hard. To her horror she found she was as excited by the challenge in his voice as she was appalled by his implication. She stood up to face him, her skin flushed with mortification and anger. She had to resist the urge to raise her own hand to her mouth and bite on it until she drew blood. To have changed overnight from a frigid, unresponsive lump of ice to a...a shameless wanton who found herself thrilling to the practised seduction routine of a man like him...it was the cruellest bit of timing on nature's part that she could imagine.

'That's a despicable thing to say. You've gone too far. Now if you'd care to leave my room I'll get Room Service to send up a snack,' she said icily.

He smiled engagingly. 'Come on, Ferry... I have to admit that I find this touchiness of yours very encouraging. But it was intended as a joke.'

Ferry bit her lip. Right at the beginning she had recognised that this simmering attraction was robbing her of her sense of humour. She must calm down a bit, or he'd win hands down.

'I...I don't see the joke, Stefan,' she said uncertainly, her face creasing into a serious frown. 'To me it just sounded...offensive. But if I'm over-reacting then I apologise.'

He came and took her by the elbow. 'Look, let's go downstairs and get something to eat here. It's been a long day... and we do need to eat, at least...' He was staring intently into her eyes as he spoke.

She looked away. 'OK,' she agreed with a resigned sigh.

There was a choice of restaurants in the hotel. He selected one with a traditional flavour, and they were led by a girl in a prettily embroidered national costume to a quiet, candlelit table where they were immediately served with apricot brandy and crudités. Stefan ordered for her—sticking to local wines and traditional Hungarian fare, including the goulash, all beautifully cooked and served. He treated the staff courteously. He spoke Hungarian softly and without a trace of bluster. He consulted her tactfully over the choice of dishes. In other words, he couldn't have been less pompous.

Throughout the meal he treated her to a dose of the same irresistible charm he had doled out to the Brussels bureaucrats. He even managed to pay the gypsy violinist to stay away from their table with an impressive degree of civility. At the banquet she had been impressed by his ability to amuse and intrigue the lugubrious diners. She was enraged by his ability to do exactly the same to her. The smiles she produced in response to his humorous remarks were all, to her disgust, perfectly genuine.

In between smiles, though, she lashed herself with renewed fury. She swallowed bile with her food, and had to keep struggling to find her very own, fraudulent smile, to wear while she thought her evil thoughts. If she let him see how disturbed she was, he'd gloat. And yet she couldn't just let herself succumb to his charm. That way lay the worst sort of humiliation. It seemed she couldn't win where Stefan Redwell was concerned.

As they retreated from the restaurant, through the busy bars towards the lift, something suddenly occurred to her. 'You've never had your nose broken, have you?' she asked unexpectedly.

He shook his head. 'Why? Are you threatening to do it for me?'

'I'd love to, as it happens. But I learned my lesson when I slapped your face.'

'So why do you ask?'

'I don't know. I sort of assumed . . . anyway, it's just that you've got a very Hungarian sort of face. I didn't realise it until I came here and saw all these other Hungarians.'

Stefan ran his fingers through his hair and loosened his tie, leaning back against the mirrored wall of the lift. She could see him from all angles, reflected into infinity. She felt weak at the knees so that merely standing was an effort—even her breathing didn't seem to be happening without a conscious effort of will. He was so powerfully built, so uncompromisingly male . . . She swallowed hard as she felt her breasts tingle and a hard bud of desire began to open deep inside her.

'I've got a Magyar bone-structure. I get it from my mother. How much else I've taken from her it's hard to tell. My romantic streak, no doubt . . .'

Ferry looked at him in disbelief. 'Romantic? You?'

He pulled a face. 'I like to think so, yes. It's certainly not an English trait. You English are about as romantic as the average wall-mounted central-heating boiler.'

'We English? Do you lump the entire race together like that?' she snapped, glad that he was being so annoying. He'd say something pompous any minute now. They emerged into their corridor.

'No. There are all sorts of different types of English people. I was simply referring to the vacuous version of Englishness that you typify. All superficial good manners, while behind it . . .' He left the sentence unfinished.

'Me?' Actually, being annoyed was making things worse. It seemed to have set her heart racing, and the blood was flowing so fast through her veins that her desire was already opening into full bloom.

He tutted and pulled an apologetic face. 'Oh, dear. That's the Hungarian in me speaking its mind again. Sorry. Let's get back to talking properly.'

'What on earth do you mean?' Even her voice was husky with awareness.

'Yes. You know... Oh, let me see... What sort of music do you like, Ferry?'

'I don't like music. I'm tone-deaf. And if you have something disparaging to say about me and wall-mounted central-heating boilers I'd rather hear it...'

'Oh, Ferry! Mendacity again? And I thought we were curing you of that!'

'I'm deadly serious. Explain what you meant.' Ferry clutched her room key in her hand, but didn't attempt to insert it into the lock.

He laughed. 'Don't you like it, Ferry, when I'm polite instead of honest? How odd. That's exactly how you behave with me most of the time.'

'Not lately, I don't.'

He frowned. 'Hmm. You certainly have improved, though I must admit I was expecting you to revert to type over the meal. You took me by surprise. That laughter of yours was quite genuine, wasn't it?' He sighed.

'It seems to me you don't know what you want from me,' she returned archly. She *had* to get away from him. She unlocked the door.

'Oh, but I do...' he said in a voice so low that it was almost a growl. And then he leaned across her and caught hold of the door-handle in one sinuous, leonine movement. 'I want you to stop playing your games and start playing mine.'

His shoulder brushed against her breasts, making her gasp with a kind of shock. His hair was close to her face, so unbelievably thick and—close to—streaked with every shade from honey through gold to pale blond. She could smell his skin behind the fresh, clean scent of soap. She pressed her back against the door-frame, trying to shrink away from him. But there was too much of him. The inch she achieved, clenching her stomach muscles hard against the soft, yielding warmth of her need, was not enough. He was straightening up, the door held wide, and his big hand was moving gently to her shoulder and ushering her in. She *had* to go where he led. That or scream, and she didn't really feel like screaming in a hotel corridor in Hungary.

She walked straight across to the glass doors. Someone had been in her room and had closed the curtains. She threw them back.

'Ah, good,' she said in a silly, light voice. 'The view . . . it's wonderful.'

'It's pitch-black out there.'

'The lights,' she said. 'They remind me . . . of . . . of the view.'

'Did you think it might have disappeared?' he asked laconically, closing the door and idly sauntering across the room to the cream leather sofa, and sitting down.

Ferry leant her back against the cold glass. She felt a little better now that she had put some distance between them. She watched him unknotting his tie and undoing the top button of his shirt.

'Why have you come into my room, Stefan?' she asked guardedly.

He took off his tie with an impatient, tugging movement. 'I thought you wanted to know about wall-mounted central-heating boilers?'

'So you've just come in here to insult me?'

He smiled his smile of unremitting charm. 'No. I don't really want to insult you. Not now. Not at this time of night.'

She folded her arms across her aching breasts, horrified at the way they were thrusting against her camisole, as if trying to attract his attention. 'Then why? Are you planning to seduce me?'

He let his head drop back against the top of the sofa and laughed. The sinews in his neck tautened. 'What's the problem, Ferry?' he asked slowly. Then he reached one arm over the back of the sofa and drew a trolley towards him. She hadn't noticed it before. It was covered in flowers, and bore an ice bucket containing a bottle of champagne.

'You *are* planning to seduce me,' she muttered accusingly.

But he shook his head. 'Not seduce, exactly. Though I would like to make love with you.'

'But not seduce me...?' One corner of her mouth tightened in sharp disapproval. Her stomach flipped over.

'No. I'm afraid I don't agree with the idea of seduction. It rather implies that one party at least is less than willing.'

'So you like your conquests to be effortless?' she taunted.

He raised his eyebrows quirkily. 'You make me sound lazy, Ferry, and I can assure you that I am a most attentive lover. There is nothing effortless about the way I make love.'

Ferry clenched her thighs together. Her stupid, inexperienced body was loving every minute of this. She wanted to claw at her skin—to punish herself for this unwelcome response. Instead she just hugged her folded arms even tighter against her breasts. 'Go away, Stefan,' she said coldly. 'I am about as unwilling as a woman can be. You're wasting your time.'

He sat forward, resting his elbows on his knees and smiling. The jacket of his suit was stretched tight across his muscular shoulders. 'Oh, I doubt I'm wasting *anything*,' he said equably. 'It's simply that I haven't wasted enough of whatever it is I have to waste . . . yet. Isn't that it, Ferry?'

Anger began to rumble inside her. 'You are the rudest man I have ever come across,' she said tightly, her eyes flashing.

He laughed. 'I know. It's because I'm only half English. That's what I was trying to explain earlier. I just don't have this formalised politeness ingrained in me. Can't you forgive me that?'

'I don't see why I should forgive you for being rude. Nor for accusing me of . . . what was it? Formalised politeness?'

'But that's exactly how you are, Ferry. You smile all the time, for a start. And I'll bet when people ask how you are you always reply that you're fine. Even if you were in the middle of having a heart attack you'd say fine.' He assumed a gratingly British falsetto. 'I'm fine. Absolutely marvellous. But I wonder—could I impose most dreadfully and ask you to ring for an ambulance for me? Oh, you can't? Never mind. No, no . . . honestly, it's fine . . .'

'I'm not like that.'

'Aren't you? How very odd. That's exactly how you come across.'

'Only to you. I have plenty of friends who think I'm . . .'

'Think you're what?'

'I was going to say "fine," ' she said bitterly.

'Ha! Then you admit that you aren't fine at all.'

'I am. I'm very happy.'

'Ferry, that's the most outrageous lie I've ever heard in all my life. You may have thought you were happy when you started working for me. But you've been getting angrier and angrier for the past ten days. If you'd been really happy to start with, a few days in my company wouldn't have disturbed you at all. Now you're about to boil over, which is great. Because it's just how I want you.'

'Want me? You don't want me at all—except to satisfy your own ego.'

'Ferry, if I were the least concerned about satisfying my ego, I wouldn't be here with you now.'

She shook her head. 'I'm not going to bother to un- ravel that insult. I've had enough. Leave my room this instant, Stefan.'

He pursed his lips in a mocking smile. 'Oh, dear. I can see I'm not about to be let off lightly.' He glanced at his watch. 'Still, it *is* getting late, and we've a lot to get through in the morning. Perhaps I'll leave the love- making until tomorrow, after all.'

And with that he stuffed his tie in his pocket and got to his feet. Then he picked up the bottle of champagne and stuck one of the flutes in his pocket. He paused and drew one thumb thoughtfully across his mouth.

'Sleep well, Ferry,' he said as he made his way across to the door.

She glowered. 'Just go away,' she said tightly. The petals began to drop, somewhere deep inside. Her stupid body was disappointed, but she herself was absolutely delighted. She'd *known* he'd brought her to Hungary for something like this. Well, regardless of the way her senses were reacting she was going to reject him and reject him again. If nothing else, she knew exactly what that did to men. It made them pompous. By tomorrow or the next day she'd be out of the mire and back on the route to happiness. Then she could go to Crete and . . . Well, at least she could try.

CHAPTER SEVEN

FERRY was horibbly restless all night. Her limbs ached for Stefan, while her heart condemned him bitterly. When she got up the next morning she showered and washed her hair with unusual vigour. She was damned if she'd let him have the satisfaction of believing he had upset her one jot the previous evening. She put on the boldest of her work skirts, a lively pillar-box red, and a fluffy white jumper over a grass-green blouse. She *loved* her freckles. They allowed her to get away with wearing the boldest colours. She never looked the least bit pale, no matter how little sleep she'd had. By the time she'd put on a sludgy olive eyeshadow and some blusher and lipstick and dried her hair, she looked terrific.

She was already downstairs, having been seated at a table overlooking the city, and tucking into some unidentifiable small fish, when Stefan arrived. He looked tousled, but his jaw shone from having been freshly shaven, and he smelled of soap. He was dressed casually in charcoal cords and a navy guernsey over a soft red shirt. She'd never seen him in casual clothes before. Infuriatingly he looked every bit as attractive. More so, in fact. He always looked confined by his suits.

She looked up, smiling brightly. 'Won't you join me? These fish are delicious—they look a bit like sardines, but I think they're fresh-water fish of some kind.'

'I'll just have coffee,' he said, giving her a smile as jagged as a saw-blade.

She sucked on her lower lip before saying cheerfully, 'Did you drink all that champagne? I *do* hope the hangover is absolutely foul.'

He glowered at her. 'As it happens, I've already had breakfast in my room.'

'Oh, dear... and I was so hoping that you'd have a dreadful headache... never mind.'

'My God, what *has* happened to you? That bloody smile used to be bad enough—but at least it used to be accompanied by soothing words. But now we've got the sickly smile *and* the lacerating tongue together. I don't think I'm going to be able to bear it.'

She sighed. 'I'm afraid it's your own fault. You insisted that I come to Hungary with you. Which means that you're just going to have to put up with both.'

'Why, for crying out loud? If nothing else, surely we established last night that the smile is superfluous. I mean, it doesn't fool me one little bit. Why bother?'

'Because you can't stand it. That's why. I can't think of one good reason for doing anything at all to please you. And you'll no doubt be disgusted to know that I've never felt so cheerful in all my life as I do today.' She smiled maliciously, and looked out of the window. 'The view is absolutely stunning, isn't it? And what blissful weather!'

Stefan folded his arms on the table and scowled at the clear blue sky, spread gaily behind the domes and spires of the old city. 'Yeah,' he sighed, catching the eye of a waitress and ordering a pot of coffee and some fruit. 'How can you bear to eat those fish this early in the morning?'

'The waitress told me they were a regional delicacy, and being so typically English I'm always terribly adventurous when I go abroad. I can't imagine why the

British have a reputation for conservatism when it comes to foreign food.'

Stefan curled his lip with disgust. 'Well, *I've* never met any Hungarians who eat that for breakfast. They'd have more sense. They smell dreadful,' he muttered.

To tell the truth, they tasted pretty fishy for this hour of the morning, but Ferry wasn't about to admit it. She dissected out the head and tail of the last fish, and put the remainder, whole, into her mouth, taking care not to gag as she swallowed. She pushed her plate away from her, making sure it was right underneath Stefan's nose. 'Delicious!' she exclaimed.

'Ferry,' he sighed, pushing the plate right over to one side of the table, 'could we call a truce?'

She blinked ingenuously. 'Truce? Whatever for?' And then before he could reply she smiled very sweetly and pointed out of the window. 'That blue there, between those trees ... that must be the Danube, surely?'

'Uh-huh.'

'And that dome—the big one ... look ... you can just see it ... is that the Parliament Building?'

He closed his eyes. 'Quite probably.'

'Don't you know?'

'I'm not a tour guide.'

'But you've been to Budapest hundreds of times. You told me all about how it used to be in the old days last night.'

He propped his jaw in his hand, his elbow on the table, and sipped at his coffee. 'Too hot,' he muttered, putting the cup back down in the saucer.

Ferry picked it up and began to blow on it. 'There!' she said, setting it back in its saucer. 'I'm sure you'll find that's better now.'

Stefan put his other elbow on the table and cupped his chin in his hands. His head butted forward and his eyes met hers keenly. 'Stop it, for God's sake, Ferry, just stop it,' he said with a peculiarly noxious smile of his own.

She smiled the smile of a Cheshire cat. 'Stop what?'

'Stop pretending.'

'But I'm not pretending, Stefan. I'm simply behaving in the way most guaranteed to irritate you. It's what I honestly feel like doing. Where's the pretence in that?'

He growled and screwed up his eyes.

'What are we doing today?' she sang out blithely.

Stefan leaned back in his chair and pushed his hair back from his face. He sighed. 'Assuming you live that long—work. But only if you stop this sunshine-and-light nonsense. Otherwise you might as well get the first flight home. If I have to try to sort out a serious problem with you chirruping like a budgie in the background you'll end up being thrown bodily through a plate-glass window.'

Ferry narrowed her own eyes. 'OK,' she said consideringly. 'It's a deal. While we're working I'll switch it off—that's if there's genuinely any work for me to do, which I doubt. But the rest of the time I shall behave exactly as I want to. And you can't do a damned thing to stop me.' And then she pointed out of the window again. 'That funny turreted thing down there—see where I'm pointing——'

Stefan's eyes snapped to. 'Shut up,' he said grimly. 'We have business to attend to. At least we do if that's the only way to stop you wittering. We're going to see Béla—that's the old man's son. The one who's a librarian. He's pulled out of this plan to start up the business again. Rosa's been to see him and she couldn't make any headway...'

'Rosa?' Ferry tucked in her angular chin and frowned. 'When was that? It's only a week and a bit since I looked at the file and nobody had been out there then.'

'Yesterday morning,' he sighed. 'Didn't I mention it? She's—er—how shall I put it? Back on the payroll. We patched things up on Tuesday evening.'

'Uh-huh,' said Ferry, holding the tip of her tongue very tightly between her teeth. So it was Rosa who'd left her nightwear scattered over Stefan's bathroom floor...? Jolly good. Excellent. No reason in the world why she should care... She hated them both. Let them do exactly as they pleased...

'Anyway, she got an early flight out yesterday to set the wheels in motion.'

'Uh-huh...' Yes. That would explain why she hadn't had time to clear up the bathroom behind her. And all those languages—stood to reason he'd use her for more than mere secretarial work... Absolutely straight-forward. Ferry bit a little too hard on the tip of her tongue, and then withdrew her tongue from between her teeth and sucked furiously to dispel the pain. She wished she hadn't eaten those fish. She felt quite queasy at the realisation that she still minded.

'Apparently it proved more difficult than we'd anticipated. The fellow isn't playing ball for some obscure reason. She's given up in despair and gone back home.'

Ferry smiled a strange, contorted smile.

'I thought I'd told you to cut that out,' Stefan ground out sharply.

Ferry shrugged. 'It's not a cheerful, irritating smile. It's a gloating smile. When you say "we" I assume you mean the royal "we". In keeping with your blood-line, no doubt. If you remember *I* predicted exactly this state of affairs...'

Stefan sighed, and she sensed an buffeting anger blow through him. 'Yes, yes, Ferry. We all know how wise a child you are... No need to rub it in. Though how you could possibly have guessed from those few letters I can't imagine.'

Nor could Ferry if the truth be known. It had been pure chance—a stab in the dark aimed simply at... well, at irritating Stefan. She hadn't progressed very far in a week and a half, had she? 'So what's his objection?' she asked with a defeated sigh.

Stefan pulled a face. 'I don't really know. He says he likes his job. He doesn't want to go back to the village— he's got a couple of kids—I suppose their education comes into it somewhere.'

'And a wife?'

'Of course.'

'Not all children are raised in two-parent families, you know,' said Ferry crossly. 'And they all sound like perfectly good reasons to me. For crying out loud, Stefan, are you really so out of touch with real people and the way they live their lives that you can't see that?'

'I said "of course" simply because his wife is a cousin of mine,' he returned coolly.

'Oh,' returned Ferry contritely. 'I didn't realise that.' To be honest, it had never occured to her that the King of the Beasts might have relatives who were craftsmen. 'I thought your mother was a princess,' she added defensively.

Stefan sighed. 'Hungarian princesses are... well, let's just say that she isn't first in line to the throne. She's about two hundred and seventy-fourth in line to nothing, if you really want to know, and that's only if you count illegitimate lines as being valid. Where did you get that piece of information, anyway?'

'Ray,' admitted Ferry, feeling very stupid. 'He...he seemed very impressed.'

Stefan's mouth curved into a wry smile. 'If you'd asked me five minutes ago whether Ray and my mother had anything in common I would have laughed. However, it's just struck me that they do, in fact, share one characteristic.' He paused. 'They're both dreadful snobs.' And then he did laugh, despite himself. A rich, humorous chuckle, which shook his big frame and set his eyes dancing. And then he laughed a bit more and said, 'Two. Didn't you say that he had bunions?'

Ferry nodded. Last night she had laughed with Stefan. He'd been so calculatingly charming and amusing that she hadn't been able to help herself—though she hadn't wanted to at all. This morning he wasn't being the least bit calculating, nor the least bit charming, but she wanted to laugh with him more than anything in the world. Even though she hated him. Because, although she'd never met Maria Redwell, she'd heard that exquisite, honeyed voice oozing down a telephone line, and that in itself was sufficient to make the comparison quite hilarious, let alone the fact that Stefan had just announced that he couldn't care less about the colour of one's blood. She didn't laugh, though. She was too determined to annoy Stefan.

Instead she said, 'Anyway, to get back to the point...which I take it has nothing to do with the fact that your mother has bunions...' She hesitated then added archly, 'Though it wouldn't surprise me to know that our visit has more to do with the state of your mother's feet than with work...'

'You are *so* opinionated,' Stefan growled, cupping his chin in his big hand and peering at her irritably. 'You seem to take a delight in refusing to take me at face value—even though I've told you already that I'm no good at your very English games. Of course we're here to work, though, as I admitted last night, I'd also like to make love with you—when you can bring yourself to concede that it's inevitable, that is.'

'Inevitable? You must be joking. It's about time you started taking *me* at face value, Stefan!'

He just gave her a sardonic smile. 'How can I, when you confessed on your very first day to hiding your real self behind a lot of simpering smiles?'

'That was when I thought you were going to turn out to be yet another boring boss.'

His eyes glittered and his mouth broke into a wide, triumphant smile. 'Ha! So you admit that you find me attractive?'

She shook her head angrily. 'Not at all. I merely admitted that you haven't been as predictible as most of my bosses . . .'

He sighed wearily. 'Are they really all the same, Ferry? Is that how you view men?'

'No!' she exclaimed sharply. 'Look—I'm a secretary. A temp. I have to be very adaptable. The people I work for—both men *and* women, as it happens—do very responsible jobs; High-Temp only accepts vacancies from people who need someone really good. Naturally, regular secretaries get to know their bosses as well-rounded people. But I don't have time to do that. My employers treat me, on the whole, in a fairly formal, distant sort of manner, and I return the compliment.' She glowered at him. 'It usually makes life easier, being polite to my employers.'

He shook his head in disbelief. 'And is that all you're interested in? An easy life? Holidays . . .' He stopped himself. 'Don't answer that,' he added. 'You'd only lie, and I don't think I could take lies on top of that breakfast of yours.' And he picked up the plate heaped with little bones and stretched out one long arm, leant back in his chair and placed it on an unoccupied neighbouring table.

Ferry watched his long, muscular frame extend lengthways in the chair. Then she watched it contract—lean; loose-limbed; relaxed—until he was facing her again, his arms folded on the table. 'Now, to get back to the matter of the Munkácsys——'

She didn't wait for him to finish. She was suddenly too uncomfortably aware of him as a man to stay silent, just watching him, any longer. It was making her very jumpy. 'As it happens, my opinion——'

'Look, if I want your opinion——'

'Damn it. You *asked* me for my opinion on this business on my very first day. I'm quite well aware that you only asked me in order to put me in my place as an empty-headed little secretary. Well, tough. I'm also aware that you're only discussing matters with me now in order to stop me annoying you by being cheerful. I'm even more aware that the only function I have on this entire trip is to provide you with a little light entertainment. After all, what am I supposed to do while you try to win the son around? Take dictation? I presume you'll be chattering to him in Hungarian so that's hardly very likely.'

'If you had heard me out you would have found that I was about to say that if I want your opinion of *my character* I'll ask for it.'

'Good. Go ahead. Because I have a few more comments on that subject I'd delight in making.'

'Later. I shall certainly take you up on that later. However, before I do I would just like to point out that your role in all this is in fact that of chatterer—not listener. I shall do any translating necessary, but as Béla speaks fluent English that shouldn't be necessary. You are here because you were the only person in a long line of people with whom I have discussed this operation who has thought to query the son's position. Everybody else— myself included, I have to agree—had assumed that the opportunity to get in on the ground floor of what promises to be a hugely lucrative business would be temptation enough. I figured that *you* had to be the best person to get to the bottom of it. Before we really understand where he's coming from we can't possibly set about changing his mind, can we?'

Ferry surveyed him sulkily. She really didn't want to be flattered by him in any way at all. She wanted him to be as arrogant as he had been the previous evening. Life would be much easier if Stefan Redwell would stick to his allotted role of dilettante playboy, without an ounce of good judgement to his name. 'You could easily have found someone else to sort it out. You just wanted me here so that you could demoralise me and seduce me. I'm just a dumb little temporary secretary, remember? Not some high-powered female executive.'

He sighed. 'If you don't want to be seduced, then I shan't be able to seduce you, shall I? If you *really* don't want to take up where we left off on Friday night, then I can't imagine why you've brought the subject up. I don't force myself on anyone, Ferry.'

She bit her lip and felt her face reddening. There didn't seem to be any answer to that.

'However,' he continued briskly. 'whether you choose to believe it or not, there are indeed very sound business reasons for my bringing you along. You have devised little mental pigeon-holes into which you slot men. I can't say that I approve of your system, but I'm prepared to concede that it works. You certainly sussed Mark and Ray out with admirable speed and accuracy. Now, unlike you, I don't categorise people like that. I may have employed you as a temp, Ferry, but I have no intention of squandering your other talents. You are here because you can be of use to my company. If you like I can re-write your job description to include this new role, and increase your salary accordingly.' He paused, then added disparagingly, 'You should be able to afford an extra week in Crete then. Though God help the poor Greeks. I don't know what they've done to deserve such pun-ishment.' There was a moment's silence. 'Does that satisfy you?'

'No. It still doesn't make sense. I may have provided the initial insight, but that doesn't mean I have to be the one to carry it through. I haven't a clue how to go about something like that...'

Stefan shook his head decisively. 'Certainly I could have found someone else. But that would have taken time. Make no mistake—matters *do* have to be sorted out quickly, Ferry. My financiers and buyers aren't going to hang on indefinitely while this guy dithers. In the meantime, other people in the business know that one of the most famous silversmiths of this century is thinking of setting up in production again. We could easily lose them to someone else if it were thought that we weren't serious. I run a tight ship, Ferry. Every company in the Redwell group has to pay its way—has to keep on being innovative and moving forward. This old man and his son are very important as far as our Bond Street outlet are concerned.'

Ferry tugged at one earlobe. Try as she might, she couldn't help but be impressed by his unexpectedly serious attitude to their mission. 'But I thought you were of the opinion that the moving of pepperpots from A to B was a fairly mundane business?' she ventured, trying to revive her feelings of animosity.

His eyes flickered coldly. 'In many ways I don't find it the most challenging of enterprises to run, certainly.

But it's highly profitable, and important in a number of other respects. I'm capable of being galvanised in its interests when the occasion demands. And I expect my employees to follow suit. Understood?'

Ferry stared at him. 'I shan't try to sabotage things, if that's what you're thinking.'

'Good.'

'And you won't try to seduce me again?'

He gave a dry chuckle. 'Ferry, I can't imagine why you're so bothered . . . All you have to do is say no, and that's the end of the matter. Why on earth don't you drop the subject?'

Ferry felt her face grow warm. 'When do we go?' she asked hastily.

'We're meeting him at ten-thirty. Unfortunately, we being such early birds, that's rather a long way off.'

'I have a good book,' said Ferry stiffly.

And then Stefan gave one of his nicer smiles and stood up very abruptly, pulling his sweater over his head as he did so. He flung it over one shoulder and then unexpectedly reached out and grabbed her wrist. 'Oh, no. You haven't come to Budapest to read a good book. I shall take you down to the banks of the river and show you the famous Danube in all its blueness. Hungarians are early risers. There'll be plenty to see.'

Ferry had frozen absolutely rigid. She stared at his hand on her sleeve. Big and powerful and it burned its imprint through her layers of clothes. She raised her other hand and began to peel back his fingers. She sensed the strength of them, and swallowed hard against the tight knot of anticipation which leapt in her throat. 'Don't touch me,' she said in a low, muffled voice. 'Don't touch me, Stefan . . .'

He took his hand away. His eyes widened, and his mouth curled wryly. 'Don't you like being touched all of a sudden?' he said softly.

She ran her tongue over her lips. Oh, no. Unfortunately the clock had not turned itself back. Anything but. All the little hairs on the back of her neck were standing on end, and her nipples rubbed almost painfully against the inside of her bra. His touch had been like a burst of electricity, charging up her with nagging desire. Even after all the things he'd said—despite Rosa being back in the picture—she could still react to him like this! She was appalled.

The air outside was sharp, despite the warmth of the spring sunshine. She was glad. It meant she could keep on her chunky white parka while she was sitting at the riverside café, and hide in its bulk. Stefan, who seemed perpetually infuriated by the presence of his own clothes, took off his leather jacket, though, and tossed it across a chair. The city was astonishingly beautiful, and still wonderfully unspoiled and uncluttered by tourists.

Stefan was in a relaxed good humour, just as he had been at dinner the previous evening. He shared a joke with the girl who served him, and engaged a couple of old men at a nearby table in animated conversation. Ferry sank deeper into her gloom. Stefan couldn't be less pompous if he tried.

At last he looked at his watch and pronounced it time to go. 'We'll walk,' he said. 'It's not far.'

'Aren't you going to go back to the hotel and change?' she asked.

'Change?' he looked surprised, and then he barred his teeth and growled, 'What into? A werewolf?'

'You did that last night,' she muttered.

Stefan laughed. 'No, I didn't. I drank a whole bottle of champagne all by myself last night. Not to mention a few whiskies from the mini-bar in my room. It turned me into a bear with a sore head. Definitely not a werewolf.'

'You said you didn't have a hangover,' she said accusingly.

He smiled, the borders of his nose doing whatever it was that they did when he was amused. 'It didn't last,' he agreed. 'Due entirely to your encouragement, I might add.'

She eyed him suspiciously. 'You sound cheerful,' she remarked.

And then he threw back his head and let out a great bellow of laughter. 'Don't you like it, Ferry? Does it irritate you?'

She sighed bitterly. 'No,' she lied.

'My cheerfulness has nothing to do with pretence, though, and everything to do with the fact that I'm in the most beautiful city on earth with a quite extraordinary woman at my side.'

'Mendacity!' she exclaimed, but he only laughed again. 'And you still haven't answered my question.'

'About changing? No. I'm not going to change. We're going to Béla's home for this discussion. I don't put on one of my Savile Row suits to call on cousins. Business suits are all about power. This business call has a good deal more to do with friendship...'

'Oh...' said Ferry. She fell silent. They were walking through the streets now, heading up a steep hill. Stefan suddenly put one heavy arm around her shoulder.

'Onward and upward,' he said.

Ferry squirmed. 'I told you not to touch me...'

'I'm not touching you,' he returned. 'My sheepskin-lined leather sleeve is resting on your cotton jacket.' He wiggled his hand at the wrist. 'My naked flesh is totally surrounded by air.'

Ferry swallowed. She didn't want her attention drawn to his hands. 'Even so...' she protested.

'Look, Ferry, I am not going to ravish you on the streets of Budapest. It's a wonderful, crisp spring morning, and my arm feels tired and your shoulder is just the right height to support it. Most women are too short to be of any use to me. You should be glad of the opportunity to help. So where's the problem?'

'I don't trust you. You're up to something.'

He smiled cynically. 'We established last night that if you're not selling then I can't buy. I don't force myself on *anyone*.'

'You're about to force yourself on Béla. You want him to bend to your will.'

Stefan withdrew his arm. 'Not force, Ferry. Find out what his problem is, and see if there isn't a solution which will keep us both happy. Pretty much the same as my intentions towards you, as it happens, now I come to think of it.'

'Liar,' she muttered. 'You don't want me happy. You've been telling me that one way and another from the moment we met.'

And then Stefan let out another huge, good-natured laugh. 'Clever girl,' he growled, his eyes sharp gold in the morning sun. 'You're right. I don't want you to be the least bit happy. Perhaps you *are* wise, after all...'

Luckily they had arrived. They stopped in front of a splendid town house dating from the last century, with heavy eaves and wrought-iron balconies in front of the upstairs windows. It was surrounded by a tangle of greenery.

Ferry looked at it in surprise. 'Golly. It's not the sort of place I would have expected a librarian to live in,' she said.

Stefan shrugged. 'It was built for my great-great-grandfather. I aquired it a couple of years ago and had it split into a couple of apartments. Béla and his family live in one half, an old aunt in the other.'

Ferry looked unblinkingly at him. 'There must still be some wonderful investment properties to be found in Eastern Europe...'

When Stefan met her eyes she was astonished to discover a cold distaste lurking in their depths. 'Oh, no,' he contradicted her steadily. 'It cost me a great deal more than it was worth. It was being used as offices. I had to rehouse the occupants before doing all the work. I shan't make a penny out of this old place, Ferry. Sorry to have to disappoint you.'

Ferry coloured. He had made her feel ashamed of herself for assuming he was materialistic. And yet everything about the man proclaimed that that was *exactly* what he was. Or at least that was how he had seemed until this morning...

Béla was a mild-mannered man of around forty. His wife was plump with curling brown hair. She smiled very warmly, chattering in Hungarian, as she ushered them into a grand drawing-room, which was sparsely but comfortably furnished with an assortment of shabby items. In the window stood a spanking-new computer. Then she hurried off to fetch them small glasses of unbelievably potent coffee and little home-baked cakes.

Stefan and Béla exchanged a few good-natured remarks, before Stefan turned to Ferry and said, 'Béla, can I leave Ferraleth with you? You won't mind if I sneak off to the kitchen and give Anna a hand clearing up, will you? I want to catch up on all the family news...'

Béla smiled his compliance. 'Ferraleth...' he said, when Stefan had left the room. 'What a beautiful name!

I haven't heard it before . . . I thought all English women were called Elizabeth or Margaret.'

Ferry grinned. She liked Béla enormously. 'Not *all*,' she said. She took a deep breath. She really didn't know where to begin. 'Look, Béla,' she sighed at last. 'Stefan expects me to try to talk you into joining forces with your father in re-establishing your old family firm. That's why he's left us alone. But . . . well, I'm afraid I'm not the negotiating type . . . I don't really know how to begin . . .'

Béla smiled humorously. 'That other one—Rosa— she's already been here on that errand. But I won't be persuaded. So why don't we talk about something else instead?'

Ferry shook her head. 'No. I've got a better idea. If I promise not to try to persuade you, why don't you just tell me exactly why you don't want to be a silversmith? Then I can convince Stefan on your behalf, and presumably he'll drop the idea then.'

Béla frowned. 'And what would Stefan have to say about that?'

Ferry shrugged. 'I don't know,' she said uncertainly. 'But we can't just talk about the weather. It would be cheating. I honestly shan't try to pressure you, though. You see, I can quite understand if you don't want to follow in your father's footsteps. I've made a similar decision myself in my own life . . . I'm on your side . . .'

It was the right *and* the wrong thing to have said. Béla laughed and explained that in fact he loved working with precious metals, and was proud of everything the old man had taught him. He explained how, in years gone by, they had melted and re-melted the small store of silver and gold they had, taking photographs which they developed themselves as the only record of the beautiful objects they had crafted. His objection was quite different. His father had taught him the value of taking a pride in one's work—no matter what that work might be. As a medical librarian he had taken a great interest in the research work which went on in Hungary—which had been conducted with a different approach from that used by doctors researching in Western countries. Now that history had thrown West and East back together again, he was trying to do the same for certain areas of research material. He was busy amalgamating a huge amount of information on computer, so that researchers across the world could have access to a broader spectrum of ideas. The project ate up all his spare time.

'There's just not time enough to do both, Ferraleth,' he said with a regretful sigh.

'Did you tell Rosa that?' queried Ferry.

He pulled a face. 'She didn't want to listen. Only to talk.' He sighed. 'It's a shame. I would so much love to do both—and yet where are the hours in the day to come from? I have gone so far with my cataloguing work now—I can't just abandon it...'

CHAPTER EIGHT

IT WAS lunchtime when they finally set off back to the hotel. Ferry couldn't help glancing repeatedly at Stefan as they walked. He had astonished her. He'd been so genuinely warm and understanding with both his cousin and Béla. And he had proved exceptionally knowledge-able about computers—even going so far as to examine Béla's work in machine code. His understanding was sufficiently profound to enable him to see exactly how Béla could be helped by the gift of a completely new computer system and a couple of programmers—whom he promised to have sent out from England, on full salary and expenses. He didn't try to *persuade* Béla of any-thing. He simply opened up the conversation in a way that let the man realise that his metalwork skills were far more unique than his computer skills. In other words, he gave Béla the hours in the day, without leaving him feeling that he had betrayed his work as a librarian.

'You didn't need me and my pigeon-holes, after all,' she commented wryly.

Stefan shrugged. 'They didn't tell Rosa any of that stuff.'

'No, well, Rosa's exceptionally——' Ferry bit her tongue. 'This weather is gorgeous, isn't it?' she finished.

'Rosa's exceptionally what?'

Ferry raised her eyebrows and looked him in the eye. 'Really,' she said. 'Does it matter? I've only met her for a matter of minutes. I don't know anything about her...'

'I can't imagine you'd let a little thing like that prevent you from forming an opinion, Ferry. Anyway, I'd very much value an outsider's view.'

'Not mine, you wouldn't,' said Ferry firmly, not a little shocked at his disloyalty. Whatever was going on between him and Rosa had to be reasonably serious. He might be more committed to his work than she had given him credit for, but didn't Stefan have *any* principles when it came to his personal life?

'Ferry...' he pronounced warningly.

She wiped the sour frown off her face and turned to him with an air of sunny innocence. They weren't talking about work any more, after all. 'Well, Rosa's exceptionally beautiful. And that yellow suit she was wearing when I saw her was exceptionally stylish. And her hair is exceptionally lustrous. And she's obviously exceptionally good at languages... You can take your pick, can't you? The list is endless.'

Stefan stuffed his hands in his trouser pockets. His brows gathered in a harsh, disapproving frown. 'How very polite and how very untruthful you can be at times, Ferry.'

She shrugged. 'Really?' she countered feebly. She didn't like being looked at like that—by anyone.

'Let me guess what you were about to say,' he continued caustically. 'Rosa's exceptionally—uh—snooty? No, you wouldn't use a word like that, would you? Um...let's see...condescending? Overpowering? Self-centred?'

Ferry eyed him balefully. Of course, it didn't mean that *Stefan* saw Rosa that way—merely that he had guessed that that was how Ferry saw her. She tried not to be pleased.

'Exceptionally impressive...?' she suggested brightly.

His eyes drooped. 'How long are you going to keep this up? If you think that Rosa's exceptionally impressive then I'm a Dutchman. You're jealous.'

'I'm not,' muttered Ferry angrily. She wasn't. Well, she was, actually, but then he was the only man she'd ever met in her life who had the power to awaken her sexual responses. She'd have to be a saint not to be jealous on a crude, animal sort of level. But that was *all*. Stefan was... She sighed. Stefan didn't actually seem to be any of those things just at present. The Hungarian air must be agreeing with him. It certainly wasn't making him pompous.

'Oh, stop lying,' he said evenly.

'We're not working any more. I told you I'd only call a halt to my air of unrelenting cheerfulness while we were working,' she muttered sourly.

Stefan made an irritable sucking noise and then said, 'Well, I was going to suggest we take the afternoon off and take a river cruise on the Danube, or maybe sample the spa facilities of the hotel. I'm told they do a really luxurious health treatment, and there's a hot mineral swimming-pool, saunas, massages and so on... But in the circumstances I think we'd better press on up to the village and see the old man.'

Ferry sighed. A river cruise on the Danube? Now that sounded just like the sort of occasion that would bring out any rejected man's most pompous instincts...

'That's fine by me,' she said stiffly. 'I'm here to work.'

Stefan smiled drily. 'You can always change the rules,' he said slyly.

But Ferry shook her head. 'No. I didn't come here to take a mud bath.'

'It'll mean no lunch if we're to make it in time,' he goaded.

'Fine. I'm not here for the free lunches, and anyway, I'm told there's no such thing...'

Stefan returned her smile coolly. 'Quite right, my girl. I shall make you pay one way or other for every last morsel you consume at my hands...'

Ferry glanced across at him. That look of cold disdain was back on his face. 'What do you think I'm playing at now, Stefan?' she asked abruptly.

He surveyed her through half-closed eyes. 'Don't you know? Of course you do. So shall I accuse you of mendacity or stupidity?'

She threw him a hostile glance. 'I *don't* know what you're talking about as it happens. As far as I'm concerned my behaviour is quite straightforward. I dislike you and I'm showing it wherever possible.'

'Then I shall have to opt for stupidity,' sighed Stefan, hailing a cab. They remained silent until they were back at the hotel.

'Go on up to your room and freshen up,' he said. 'I'll see you back here at the main entrance in half an hour.'

He was twenty-three minutes late. Ferry sat and pretended to read her fat book.

He made no comment about his late arrival, merely ushered her out to a hire car and drove off. After a while, as they began to leave the built-up areas behind them, he said, 'Undo your seatbelt and scrabble around on the back seat, Ferry.'

'Why?'

'There are a couple of packets of sandwiches under my jacket.'

She shifted his heavy leather jacket and secured the package, then opened them and handed him one.

'Mmm,' she said, taking a bite. 'This is delicious.'

Stefan took a huge bite out of his own and chewed silently for a minute, then said, 'The hotel provided them at no extra charge.'

'Ah-ha... A free lunch, after all...' she grinned in reply. 'Then I shall relish them all the more.'

He didn't reply, and she didn't mind. It was too fascinating, watching the pretty landscape unfold. It was an unspoiled world of rolling hills and woodlands, sparkling brooks and darting birds, all clothed in the fresh colours of spring, peppered with quaint farmhouses and outbuildings. They passed through a number of villages and picturesque small towns, which had Ferry craning her neck to see more, and longing to explore.

The Munkácsy seniors lived in a small timber house set on the borders of a quiet village. A big-hoofed working horse was plodding up the main street, pulling a cart laden with produce, and led by an old man in a felt hat. Ferry longed to ask a hundred questions, but, mindful of her assertion that she was here to work, she kept her mouth firmly closed and followed Stefan to the door.

Mr and Mrs Munkácsy were both nearing sixty, and neither spoke a word of English. They were one as effusive and voluble as the other, and clearly delighted to see Stefan. Their hospitality spilled over to Ferry, whom they hugged warmly and kissed on both cheeks.

'They're saying hello,' translated Stefan with a wry air.

'Tell them hello back,' grinned Ferry.

To her astonishment she found herself being introduced surname first. Lyon Ferraleth. How extraordinary. She'd never made the connection before. Though why should she? Because they certainly weren't two of a kind...

Time sped by, as the older couple chattered away, and pulled out stacks of photographs of silverware to show them. Stefan talked seriously to them, occasionally translating bits for Ferry to take down in shorthand. They went to visit the old stone workshops behind the house, which were dilapidated and old-fashioned. Even though Ferry couldn't understand much of what was going on it was clear that Stefan was outlining his plans—to the evident delight of their host and hostess.

At last they settled back into the cluttered but cosy sitting-room, where a wood-burning stove had Stefan peeling off his guernsey and rolling back the sleeves of his red shirt. Ferry continued taking notes while she roasted, and exchanged smiles with the beaming Mrs Munkácsy. Eventually the older woman disappeared into the kitchen, calling them through after a while to come and eat.

The meal was homely but delicious, and both visitors enjoyed generous portions. The local wine, full-bodied and fruity, which accompanied the meal was equally welcome. When they finally finished eating, they returned to the sitting-room to drink more tiny glasses of bitter black *kávé*.

'Shouldn't we go, Stefan?' Ferry murmured finally, glancing meaningfully at her watch.

He shrugged. 'We're staying the night...sorry...I thought I'd translated that bit...'

'Staying? You know perfectly well you didn't translate that bit. Honestly, Stefan...we can't stay. I haven't brought any things.'

He pulled a face. 'Nor have I. But I expect we'll manage.'

'No,' she returned insistently.

But Stefan just threw her a challenging smile. 'We *have* to stay,' he said. 'The drink-driving laws are exceptionally stringent here in Hungary. I come here often, and I've no intention of losing my right to drive over here. Anyway, it would be dangerous.'

'You're *very* far from being drunk. You've only had a couple of glasses of wine.'

'Hungarian law stipulates not a single drop. Anyway, I've got a very weak head . . .'

'Judging by the amount you drank last night without even a headache to show for it, that can't be true.'

'Ferry! Don't tell me you're accusing me of mendacity again?'

She felt a charge of anger build inside herself. Stefan was up to something—although she couldn't see how he could try to seduce her in this small house, with the Munkácsys present. Even so, his taunting manner warned her to resist falling in with his plans. 'Isn't there a hotel in the village? I could walk . . .'

'No. And anyway, your working brief does not include upsetting the very people we are here to appease. They would be offended. They'd think their home wasn't good enough for you. I won't let you offend them.'

If she'd believed for one moment that he was telling the truth she'd have been impressed. But he *was* up to something. Of that there could be no doubt. She glared furiously at him, then switched expressions as Mrs Munkácsy came into the room, holding out fresh towels and beaming.

'You planned this, didn't you?' she said with a happy smile, nodding at her hostess, and taking one of the plain white towels.

'Yes,' said Stefan, and when she looked at him she realised that he was playing her game now. He was smiling genially at their hosts, as if they were having the most amiable of exchanges.

'But why?'

'Wait and see... Anyway, I thought you were in favour of practical jokes...'

'I told you that I had no part in Gerry's stupid prank.'

'Technically, yes, but in fact it had everything to do with you, as well you know...'

It was hard work, keeping the smile in place. Her face was aching, her stomach churning. 'Do you go to this much trouble to offend every temp you ever employ?'

'Oh, no. Of course not. I'm very selective about whom I offend.'

They were following Mrs Munkácsy now up the narrow wooden staircase, coming to halt on a tiny square landing. Three doors opened off it. Only two were flung wide for their inspection. There was an extremely old-fashioned bathroom, very cramped, and a single bedroom with a high double bed.

The third door must conceal the Munkácsys' bedroom. Ferry looked over her shoulder. There was nothing else up here at all. Like another guest room. She gulped.

'Thank you.' She beamed at the plump woman, nodding and bowing her gratitude.

Stefan also was smiling his disarmingly charming smile, and then said a few words in Hungarian, at which Mrs Munkácsy laughed merrily, before setting off down the stairs. Ferry marched into the bedroom.

'I'll take the bed,' she snapped. 'You can take the bath.'

'No chance. We'll share the bed.'

'Don't be so stupid!'

'I'm not being stupid. Merely polite.'

'You mean they'd be offended if they thought we weren't making—er—having sex under their roof? Is it a quaint Hungarian custom to throw strangers into the same bedroom for the night?'

'We're not strangers.'

'Oh, yes, we are.'

'But I know you so well, Ferry.'

'You don't!' she exclaimed frantically. 'But that wasn't what I meant, anyway. I meant why on earth have they put us both in this room when we are neither of the same—er—gender, nor married?'

'It's the only spare room they have.'

'I gathered that, but even so...'

Stefan's eyes glittered a dark amber. 'Well, to be honest, they think we're engaged. And I'm afraid, like most people whose knowledge of Western morality comes from what they read in the papers, they think that we must therefore be—er—more intimate than is...ah...perhaps the case. They don't want to seem unsophisticated in our eyes.'

Ferry clenched her fists with annoyance. 'Why on earth did you tell them we were *engaged*?'

'I didn't.'

'Then who did?'

'Rosa, I should imagine...'

'But they haven't met her, have they?'

'No. But I believe she must have said something of the sort to Béla, who must have passed the information on.'

'Why on earth should Rosa have said that——?' And then Ferry rolled her eyes and sighed. Of course. Béla would have told his parents that Stefan was engaged to his secretary—namely Rosa—and when *she* was introduced as Stefan's secretary they had jumped to the obvious conclusion.

She glared at Stefan. Then she decisively opened the door and went downstairs. The friendly couple smiled warmly at her.

'I'm not...' she began helplessly and then splayed her fingers and offered her hands for inspection. 'No rings,'

she said, pointing to the fourth finger of her left hand.
'Look. No rings....' and she shook her head and pointed
again.

Mrs Munkácsy laughed and then put her arm around
Ferry in an unexpected hug. When she broke away she
linked the little fingers of both hands together and
nodded, as if to say, You're close enough... we don't
mind...

Ferry gave what she hoped was a cheerful smile and
went back upstairs. Stefan was sitting on the edge of the
bed, wearing nothing but his trousers.

'Put your shirt back on,' she said stiffly, closing the
door behind her.

Stefan slowly twisted around and lifted his legs up on
the bed. He lay back on the pillows, stretching his long
legs out in front of him, and linking his fingers behind
his neck.

Ferry felt a hot colour sweep across her face. His chest
was covered in more of those wiry, golden, curling hairs.
They tapered towards his navel. She wanted to lay her
hands on them and stroke them, and feel the heat of his
golden skin beneath her palms. She dragged her eyes
upwards, flinching as she met the sardonic expression
in his eyes. Stretched out there, bare-chested, relaxed,
he seemed utterly animal and utterly male. Angrily she
tossed her head and looked out of the window, but the
night beyond had turned the window into a mirror. In
the glass all she could see was another Stefan. Her heart
was jumping in her chest, and she could feel the pulse
in her neck throbbing.

'Did you know they only had one guest room?'

'Not at first. It was mentioned during the conversation, though.'

'You've got to do something,' she demanded, but her
voice shook when she spoke.

He narrowed his eyes. 'Is that an invitation?' he asked.

'No. Of course it isn't.'

He began to unbuckle the belt of his trousers.

'Stop it,' she hissed. 'For goodness' sake, stop it!'

Stefan smiled slowly. 'What's the matter, Ferry? Are you bothered by the idea of sharing a room with me for the night?'

'Of course I am! Is that so surprising?'

The fingers of one hand were still toying with the buckle in a desultory fashion. All the muscles in his big arm had tightened to the task.

'Yes. On the whole I'd say it was...'

Ferry had to struggle to make sense of what he was saying. Quite frankly, her entire consciousness was directed at the sight of Stefan, half naked and threatening to become even more so at any minute. 'Well, you've got me wrong. I'm not in the habit of sharing my bed.'

'And I've told you, Ferry. If you don't want to give, then I can't take. So what's the problem?'

'I... Simply sharing a bed is a problem.'

'Not if you *simply* turn your back on me and go to sleep.'

'I...I... That's exactly what I plan to do.'

A smile spread lazily across his features, though his eyes remained hard. 'Really?'

'Really,' she repeated insistently, focusing her eyes on his chin in the hope that it would prove neutral territory. He swallowed. His Adam's apple moved seductively in his throat. She turned her eyes up to the ceiling. 'And I can't imagine why you should think otherwise.'

'Because you want me to make love with you.'

'I don't!'

'Liar...' he breathed softly.

'I'm not,' she murmured, but her voice was weak with desire.

Stefan shrugged. His broad shoulders moved against the bank of white pillows, and the hollows around his solid collarbone deepened and then just as fleetingly disappeared. Ferry brought up a hand to cover her eyes. She scratched at one temple to disguise the purpose of the gesture, and then caught herself peeping through her fingers. Oh, God. She couldn't take her eyes off him. He hadn't touched her and already her bones were turning to water, and inside she felt a burning heat smouldering in her loins. Her knees felt weak. She felt her legs begin to tremble. She badly needed to sit down if she was to retain any semblance of composure. Hastily she searched the room with her eyes, but the only piece of furniture beside the bed was an old fashioned tallboy.

'What are you going to do?' she demanded shakily.

But Stefan just raised one eyebrow quirkily, and the borders of his nostrils quivered as he relished his silence.

She swallowed hard against a dry mouth. Ferry pressed her shaking fingers to her eyes. 'For goodness' sake, Stefan, what are you trying to do to me?'

His smile broadened. 'Whatever it is, I'm not having to try very hard, am I?' he asked.

Ferry sat heavily on the edge of the bed. 'Look, Stefan, I have no intention of letting you make love to me. I can't force you to drive me back to Budapest since you were so careful to take a few drinks, and I can't very well walk around the village all night. I'm stuck in this room with you. That much I can just about accept. But I don't see why I have to be put through some horrible kind of mental torture as well. Why don't you sleep on the floor, and I'll put the light out and take the bed?'

Stefan pulled a face. 'Well, it's nice to know that the sight of my bare chest constitutes a form of mental torture... but I'm afraid I can't agree to sleeping on the floor. Those boards are pretty hard. And there isn't enough bedding to split. It gets very cold in the hills at night at this time of year.'

Ferry stood up and snatched a pillow. She threw it angrily on the floor and then lay down, screwing up her eyes.

'Switch off the light,' she muttered. 'I'm exhausted.'

She stayed curled on her side on the floor, fully dressed, her eyes closed. Naturally, the light didn't go off, and the only sound was a faint, rhythmic creak of bedsprings as Stefan shook with laughter.

Later she heard him move around—use the bathroom and take off his trousers and come back to bed. At last the light went off. Ferry lay curled on the hard floor, her eyes tight closed, getting colder and colder.

There was a long, long silence and then the bedsprings creaked again. She didn't open her eyes until she felt Stefan's strong arms loop underneath her and lift her up into the air.

He radiated warmth. 'What are you doing?' she asked in an odd, dry voice.

'Putting you to bed,' he said, dropping her hard on to the mattress. Her cheek brushed against the hairs of his chest, making her almost cry out with desire.

She felt his hands finger the welt of her jumper. 'Arms up,' he instructed, but she clenched her arms tight across her chest.

'No...' she moaned.

She felt Stefan sit heavily on the bed beside her, and heard him sigh. 'Ferry,' he said, 'just take off your top clothes, there's a good girl. They'll look dreadful in the morning if you sleep in them. You can keep on your liberty bodice and your thick vest and woolly drawers and your tights. That should secure whatever virtue it is that you're trying to protect.'

She looked across at him suspiciously. All she could make out was his dark shape, and the silver glint of his thick hair in the sliver of moonlight which came through the window. Nervously she took off her skirt.

Stefan reached across and picked it up. 'And the jumper and blouse,' he said firmly.

She took off her jumper. 'I'll keep my blouse on,' she muttered.

Then Stefan laughed. 'Well, take your shoes off, for goodness' sake. And really, you might as well take off that blouse, too. What do you think I'm going to do?'

'I have no idea. But you've lied to get me this far. I don't trust you.' However, cloaked in the darkness, she did take off her blouse.

Stefan got under the bedclothes. 'It's bloody perishing,' he said. 'You must be like a block of ice after lying on that floor.'

Ferry wriggled under the bedclothes in her underwear and tights. She could feel warmth seeping temptingly across from his side of the bed. She rolled further towards her edge. 'I am,' she admitted.

It was the wrong thing to have said. He laid a single finger on her cheek to test the accuracy of her statement. She nearly jumped out of her skin.

Stefan slumped back on the pillows. 'Don't worry,' he muttered bitterly. 'You're too cold to tempt me.'

'Am I acting as if I want to tempt you?'

'Not right now, no. But you did last Friday. And on Monday morning in the office. At the moment your dignity is outraged and you're trying to prove a point. I should have taken you on a river cruise or for a swim and left this excursion till tomorrow. You'd have thawed by then.'

'It wouldn't matter how much time had elapsed, I still wouldn't have "thawed", as you put it. You really are unbearably arrogant, Stefan Redwell,' she said, feeling tears prick at her eyes. 'I hate you.'

'No, you don't.'

'I do.'

She felt him stir bedside her and then he laid his lips against her cheek and breathed, 'You don't hate me, Ferry.' And then he laid a big, warm, heavy hand on her cold breast and murmured, 'You want me...'

She smacked his hand away sharply. 'How dare you?' she whispered.

'Your breasts are hard with wanting me...'

'They're like that because I'm freezing cold,' she hissed, but the truth shook in her voice.

'Mendacity...' he whispered across the darkness.

'All right,' she acknowledged furiously. 'I'm lying. But what else am I supposed to do in the circumstances?'

'Then you concede that you find me attractive?'

She swallowed hard. She just couldn't keep up this act any longer. 'Yes, as a matter of fact I do. Which is why I was responsive to your kisses. But I'll *never* allow it to go any further, Stefan.'

'Really?'

'Yes, really.' Tears clotted in her throat. 'Because I may respond to you physically—quite frankly that's beyond the control of my conscious mind—but I don't respect you, Stefan. I don't like you and I don't respect you.'

There was a long silence. Ferry tried hard to control the silent tears which kept escaping from beneath her tightly closed eyelids. Then Stefan's hand came to rest comfortingly on her hunched shoulderblade. 'Don't cry, Ferry,' he said softly. 'Please don't cry.'

When she didn't reply he took his hand away and then she felt him turn over. He rolled to his edge of the bed. The space between them yawned. After a while she heard the pattern of his breathing change. He was asleep. Well, she had rejected him again. It only remained to see what the morning would bring. Their work in Hungary was finished, and her fortnight as a temp was up. If he didn't get pompous in the morning she was sunk.

Ferry felt tears clot in her throat. She wanted to make love with him so badly. But she wouldn't let herself. And suddenly she ached at the idea of her future stretching ahead of her, with no Stefan, and all those doors closing one by one.

The following morning they arose early, and were given a large breakfast before setting off. They stopped at the hotel to collect their bags, then went straight to the airport. Stefan was curt and distant. So was Ferry. Back at Heathrow she insisted on making her own way home. Her cheque, she was assured, would be deposited with Angela promptly, and would take into account the extra hours she had put in plus expenses. She could afford to go to Crete just as soon as she could get a flight.

CHAPTER NINE

CRETE was everything she had expected it to be. It also proved to be desperately lonely and dispiriting. She thought of nothing but him. She hardly ever smiled. She hated herself.

When she got back to her flat after the long, grimy journey it was late in the evening. Her mother's lights were off and the phone was ringing.

'Ferry?'

'Hi, Angela.'

'Look, Stefan wants to see you in his office; eight o'clock tomorrow morning.'

'Forget it.'

'No. He says it's important. This is my firm, Ferry, and I'm not allowing you to get away with damaging its image.'

'Its image will be a lot worse off if I go, Angela. I can promise you that.'

'Just be there.' Angela slammed down the phone.

Ferry punched one of her shabby nylon suitcases so hard that her hand hurt. There was a tap at her door. Drat. It would be her mother. Presumably she had just got back from an extra-late session at the office.

Her mother was wearing Ferry's Jean Muir dress, and was giggling a little. 'Can we come in?'

'We?'

A pair of warm, maternal arms wrapped themselves around Ferry's shoulders. 'Oh, Ferry!'

Her mother never hugged her. *Never*. How much had the woman had to drink, for goodness' sake? She seemed as high as a kite. 'Mum...?'

'Ferry, I want you to meet your father...'

So, at the age of twenty-five, Ferry met her father. He was very tall and thin, and he had nut-brown hair, poker-straight, and serious grey eyes and an angular chin and his smiling lips were as freckled as his smiling face.

When she disappeared into the red belly of the bus the following morning, she was still in shock. He had taken her completely by surprise. He was so disarmingly nice and funny and kind. He and her mother kept looking soppily into each other's eyes. They both told a similar tale of painful misunderstanding, and undying love. Twenty-five years of it, to be precise. It seemed it could take an awfully long time to fall out of love.

'You reminded me of him so much,' her mother had said at one point. 'And I loved you so much. I was frightened to let you grow up and leave me. It would have been like losing the last shred of him. But I forced myself... I threw myself into my work and kept bright and cheerful for you and encouraged you to be independent... I did right, didn't I, Ferry?'

'You did fine, Mum,' Ferry had said huskily, pasting on her cheerful smile for what she vowed would be the very last time.

Stefan was sitting in her chair, in her office, his shirt-sleeves rolled back, waiting for her.

'What's happened to Rosa?'

'I sacked her. She was so patronising with the Munkácsys. It was no good. She was great when it came to sucking up to rich clients, but she rubbed too many people up the wrong way.'

Oh, no. She was not pleased. Because if that was his version of true love, then he had a lot to learn. Just consider how much her parents had had to forgive each other, after all... 'Look, Stefan, she probably just comes from the sort of background where——'

'Why are you defending her? Don't you remember how hard she tried to put you down that first day when you typed those Russian letters?'

'One was Polish.'

'Ah, yes, I remember you pointing that out at the time. You were brilliant.'

Ferry frowned hard, trying to force the hot colour in her cheeks into abeyance. 'Why did you want to see me?'

Stefan's eyes raked lazily over her face. 'Angela tells me you're free.'

'You already knew that,' she snapped. 'I sacked Gerry a long time ago.'

The dark pupils in his golden eyes sharpened. He glared at her. '*Workwise.*'

She glared back. 'Forgive me my mistake. Only, being so cheerful, superficial and bland, I assumed that work would be the last thing on your mind.'

'Then you *are* free.'

'No. I'm not.'

'Liar.'

'Yes. If you like, I am. Now if there's nothing else you want I'll be——'

'You're coming to Sheffield with me.'

'*Liar.*'

He stood up and gripped her arm. 'Work, Ferry. That's all I want you for. Understood?'

'Huh!' She shook him off.

'A very serious crisis has blown up—almost literally, as it happens—in the Sheffield plant. I need a good secretary who understands me and can work under pressure.'

'Candice?'

'She's far too busy. And her shorthand's not up to it.'

'Use a dictation machine.'

'We'll be working in the plant some of the time: too much background noise. Now I'll take you back to your flat and you can collect a few things.'

'We've played this scene before. This time I'm changing the ending. No chance.'

He looked furiously into her eyes, stooping a little to meet her face squarely. And then he bellowed, 'Work! Work! It's really very important!'

'Moving pepperpots from A to B?' she said stiffly.

'No! God-damn it, Ferraleth, this is serious...' He ran one hand angrily through his rumpled hair. 'We've got a furnace up there—it's overheated. And we've got to put out a consignment of a special alloy for a government defence contract right away. I've got to get it sorted out as soon as possible. Like now.'

'You didn't care much when that oil sheikh had to wait for his candelabra.'

'Of course I didn't! It was a bloody candlestick! Anyway, with those sort of frilly items, the longer people have to wait, the greater they value them. But this is different. There's a whole chain of firms waiting for this consignment of steel, Ferry. Skilled workers—bread-winners—people who could be made redundant if we fail to deliver on time. It's a very big contract. It's important.'

There was a loaded pause. Ferry's heart was thundering. Then, 'You mean the entire defence of the realm rests squarely on my shoulders?'

His eyes lit up. His nostrils quivered. 'Yes.'

She sighed. She narrowed her eyes. '*Work*? That's all?'

'Work, Ferry,' he said, standing up and shrugging on his jacket. 'Now come on. We haven't a moment to waste.'

In the car she said, 'If this is so important, why didn't you go up to Sheffield last night? Why did you wait till this morning?'

'I only heard about the furnace an hour ago.'

'But Angela rang me last night.'

'Yes. Well. I wanted to see you, anyway.'

'Why?'

'To offer you Rosa's job.'

'I don't believe this.'

'Oh, damn it, Ferry, stop pretending. It's what you wanted.'

She was about to protest when the car swung to a halt outside a restaurant. The Bacchinalean. Stefan sprinted in, leaving his car door open, and sprinted out again with a long strip of fax roll and a mobile phone in his hand.

'What on earth...?'

He handed her the fax. 'You can go through that with me later. Great restaurant. I use it as a second office. Candice always knows where to find me when I can't stand all that boring talk about pepperpots any longer.' He pulled the big car out into the traffic. 'Do you know what happened last week? This guy had ordered cutlery with sapphires set into the handles. When he took delivery his first question was, "Is it dishwasher friendly?" *Then*—you're not going to believe this—*then* he complained because the stones weren't sparkly enough. We explained that they'd had to be set deep into the handles or they'd rip your hands to shreds when you used them, and they didn't catch the light so well when they were set that way. So he thought about it and suggested putting batteries and light bulbs inside the handles so that the light shone through...' Stefan paused. 'The jeweller screamed when we told him. He just stared at us and then he opened his mouth and this awful, high-pitched wail came out!'

Ferry started to laugh. She couldn't stop. Her eyes started to run with tears. She rested her head against the glass and laughed and laughed. Through the mist of tears she could make out Stefan's profile, his keen eyes fixed on the road ahead, his brow furrowed, his mouth held in a straight line.

'It was funny,' conceded Stefan in a baffled voice. 'But not *that* funny.'

'I know,' gasped Ferry. She didn't know why she was laughing quite so helplessly, either.

A few minutes later, while she continued to quake with mirth, he said, 'I shan't bother to collect anything from my place. There's a female asleep in my bed. I don't think I can handle any extra hassle this morning.'

Ferry stopped laughing.

When they got to her flat she flung an armful of clothes into one of her shabby nylon suitcases and ran back out to the car. Stefan was tapping his fingers impatiently on the steering-wheel.

They arrived on the outskirts of Sheffield late in the morning. Stefan skirted the city, and then wove his way through streets which were obviously as familiar to him as the lines on his own hands, until they arrived at a large, modern office block, six or seven storeys high, and, compared to the London offices, absolutely enormous. The moment he had parked the Mercedes he shed his London veneer. He didn't even bother to open Ferry's door, but stood in the car park and stripped off his jacket and flung it on to the back seat of his car. Then he retrieved his briefcase from the boot, and stood impatiently, waiting for Ferry to join him, rolling back his shirt-sleeves. She found she still wanted to run her lips up and down his forearms. She bit her lips very, very hard.

They entered the building at top speed. The doorman greeted Stefan genially, but he merely nodded in response. As they waited for the lift Stefan drummed his fingers on the lift door, and pressed the button three times. Obviously he didn't like spending any more time than he had to in his provincial offices. When they arrived in Stefan's suite, he barely turned his head to acknowledge the middle-aged woman who stood up to greet him, headed straight for his desk and began pressing buttons on his computer.

Ferry approached the woman, and held out her hand with a smile. 'Hello,' she said cheerfully. 'I'm Ferraleth Lyon, Mr Redwell's temporary secretary from London.'

The motherly-looking woman smiled in return as she took Ferry's hand. 'Ah . . . Ferry,' she said. 'I recognised your voice. You always sound so cheerful. I'm Candice. Let me make you a cup of coffee.'

But she had no time to drink the coffee. Stefan began to give orders in a way she had never before seen him give orders. He was crisp, insistent, controlling. There was no room for specious charm. He got Candice to summon a variety of head of departments, and hustled them gravely into his office, gesturing Ferry to accompany them.

'Note everything said,' he muttered to her, 'and note the time every ten minutes. If we end up having to answer for this little fiasco, I want *everything* on record.'

His command was absolute. The men listened attentively, and gave information concisely when asked. Apparently it would take time to repair the furnace, and in the meantime the product would have to be turned out on a brand-new, untried furnace, designed for a

completely different job; and at top speed. Before long
all of the men were down to shirt-sleeves, bending over
the computer, working out the logistics of the exercise.
A shop-floor supervisor was summoned, and duly appeared, wiping his hands on his boilersuit. He was consulted in surprising depth. Ferry had a terrible time
keeping up with them, especially as she was unfamiliar
with the technical terms; and then they kept interrupting
each other or all started talking at once. There was no
chairman to call this meeting to order, and ensure that
everyone had their say—though she noticed that
everyone fell silent with Stefan spoke. But she managed
to get everything down somehow, making a mental note
to check out the unfamiliar words with Candice as soon
as possible.

Sandwiches appeared at regular intervals, and were
eaten on the hoof. At last the team were ready to repair
to the works. The industrial site was less than a quarter
of a mile away. Stefan led the way briskly on foot, taking
huge bites out of his cheese and pickle sandwich between comments, and rumpling his hair with his free
hand. The industrial complex was dominated by great
chimneys, burning off the waste gases of the molten
metals and their fuels.

The men huddled around the new furnace as if it were
an old friend, their discussions continuing unabated.
Ferry filled her notebook with squiggles and marks,
barely finding time to look around at the huge factory,
bursting with incomprehensible equipment, and smelling
overpoweringly of oil. High above her head yellow cranes
moved on gantries like mechanical birds.

It was nearing ten when Stefan finally took off his
hard hat and ran both hands through his hair, pushing
it back off his face, and closing his eyes briefly. 'OK,
Ferry?' he said, turning to address her for the first time

in hours. He kept his hands on his head, easing out his shoulder muscles as he did so. 'That's the lot for to-night. Let's get some sleep. We'll leave the engineers to tackle the night shift.'

His blue and white striped shirt was stained with sweat. And the plant, though ultra-modern, had left a veneer of grime on his skin. This was still the same Stefan she knew from the London office: quick-witted, impatient, determined. But here, in this context, there was some definitive purpose ordering his energy. Now he was a man of action to some effect. Instead of his day con-sisting of an effete lunch with an heiress and an exam-ination of a flow chart with a pin-striped accountant, today's project had consumed him as he had bent to examine the damaged installation, and studied the con-trols of the new furnace, swapping ideas with engineers and craftsmen, white and blue collar, co-ordinating the team which ultimately would make sure that the vital contract was met.

Ferry's heart was like lead as they strolled wearily out into the crisp night air. She knew now why Stefan hadn't been pompous so far. And she knew, too, that he never would be. He wasn't that sort of man. She wanted to cry.

'Sorry about all that,' Stefan said almost automati-cally. He sounded tired but exhilarated.

Ferry smiled regretfully. 'Don't apologise. I enjoyed it.'

'Enjoyed it?' Stefan responded doubtfully.

'Hmm. I've never been in a place like that before. It was very impressive.'

'How odd. I would have thought a woman like you would have found it all very noisy and dirty and dispiriting.'

Ferry gave him one of her more acid looks. 'Pigeon-holes?' she said.

He met her eye with a look as caustic as her own. 'Yes.'

And then, floodlit both by electricity and the flames shooting from the chimneys high above, Stefan tipped back his head to look at the sky and smiled. Ferry stood still, her eyes narrowed, watching him.

She let him get ahead of her, to get a better view. The sight of him far outshone the Acropolis at dawn. She wished now that she'd made it to India on one of her holidays. She'd never seen the Taj Mahal, and it was a shame. The comparison would have been worth making. Night was velvety black up above, but the whole site was filled with a flaring blue luminescence. It was strangely colourless. Stefan, his hair silver now, rather than its usual dusty gold, his features delineated by shade, stretched his arms high into the air, fists clenched, in something that more closely resembled a triumphal gesture than a leonine stretch. He looked especially big tonight. His shirt eased at the waistband and tightened across his solid shoulderblades, while Ferry's bones practically melted. Here, tonight, in this context, he was quite, quite splendid. She put her hands to her face. Oh…she should never have come. She just couldn't bear it.

She had fought the knowledge while she toured the sites of ancient Crete, long-faced and weary. Now she knew it beyond a shadow of doubt. She had indeed fallen in love with Stefan Redwell. She gazed and gazed at him. He wasn't the man for her. Right now in this strange light he didn't even look like a real man, anyway. More like some ancient idol, mysterious in moonlight, awaiting worship. Well, for tonight at least she felt like worshipping him from afar. He'd impressed her immeasurably since they'd arrived in Sheffield. She could allow herself the luxury of a little idolatory before she struggled with the horrors of trying to fall out of love.

He turned and started walking backwards. 'Come on!' he called.

Ferry sighed and then increased her pace to catch up with him. He kept walking backwards—needless to say he was every bit as confident in reverse gear—but he did slow down a little to let her gain on him. And then, when she drew abreast of him, he swivelled around and clapped one big hand on her shoulder, drawing her against his side.

'Good work, Ferraleth,' he said, slapping the top of her arm. 'I think we've got the worst of it sorted out. We can congratulate ourselves.'

Ferry closed her eyes and took a deep breath. Then she ducked clumsily out from his comradely embrace. Tears bit angrily at her eyes.

'Can I get a train back to London tonight?' she asked gruffly.

'No need. It's only about eight or nine miles to the family home. There's plenty of room.'

'I want to go back to London, Stefan. I really don't feel up to meeting your family tonight.'

'Good. Because none of them is at home. Which will give me plenty of opportunity to do this...' And he caught hold of the tops of her arms.

'Don't kiss me!' she cried, almost wild with anguish, struggling against the press of his fingers. She closed her eyes tight with panic. His mouth brushed roughly across hers. The brief sensation of his lips touching hers was quite sufficient to ignite that smouldering need deep inside her. She could smell the distinctive tang of his skin, feel his warmth, sense his strength. She pressed her lips together and, summoning all her will-power, turned her head resolutely to one side.

'You liked it when I kissed you before,' he said challengingly, keeping hold of her arms.

Oh, yes. But then she'd been kissed by the lion rampant; the man who wanted to prove that he was irresistible to secretaries. Ultimately, that man had proved resistible—just. Stefan, smelling of fresh sweat and triumph, his shirt creased, monochrome against the night sky, seemed altogether another animal. She ached with love for him. She couldn't bear the idea of making herself resist this man against all the force of her massed instincts.

'No...no...' she protested, trying to wrench her arms away, but his grip just tightened slightly. She could hardly breathe. Her breasts hardened expectantly. 'No...' she said again.

They were facing each other now—feet scuffling, bodies bent slightly from the waist, like a pair of undernourished sumo wrestlers. Stefan's face, bleached of colour, dark hollows beneath his prominent cheekbones, tantalised her with its stark beauty. His eyes glittered like diamonds in the strange, ethereal light. They were pulling in opposite directions. All she needed to do, her inner voice coaxed, was to stop pulling. She would end up tumbling against his chest, encircled by his arms, being kissed by him all over again. Would that really be so wrong?

'Oh, let me go!' she groaned, clenching her fists and closing her eyes against the sight of him.

He let go of her very suddenly, so that she staggered backwards. When she regained her balance and looked into his face it was dark with anger.

'What do I have to do?' he asked furiously. 'I've offered you Rosa's job. I've run out of bait.'

She looked at him, her eyes wide with horror. 'What's that got to do with anything?'

'That's the bargain, isn't it, Ferry?' he asked bitterly, stuffing his hands into his pockets. He began to walk.

She caught him up and grabbed at his shirt-sleeve. 'What bargain? What are you on about?'

He put his big hands up to his face and rubbed fiercely at his brow. 'Oh, stop it. You know damned well what I mean. I know all about the kind of bartering you go in for. OK, so I should have realised that some poor sap would already have bought you the luggage. Anyone as fixated on holidays as you are would have made that an early priority. And I agree I should have found out which perfume you actually preferred; and it was tactless not to offer to pay for the hair and dress out of my own pocket, instead of the firm's. But I'm no damned good at that kind of thing, Ferry. I don't live my life by your kind of rules and I'm just no bloody good at playing the game.'

She clenched again at the striped cotton of his sleeve and shook it wildly. 'Is that what you think?' she said in a voice hoarse with outrage. 'Is that what you think I'm like? Kisses in exchange for luxury items? Do you think I'm some kind of human version of a green-shield-stamp catalogue?' Her voice rose higher and higher.

He turned his blazing eyes on Ferry. 'Unfortunately, you virtually spelled it out, Ferry. So it's just no good acting so dumb. I can't say I like your terms, but, as you're giving me no choice, I'm prepared to play along with them. Can I say fairer than that?'

She let go of his sleeve then. Impelled by a choking fury, her hands formed themselves into claws, which she waved ineffectually in front of her face. 'Spelled it out?' she echoed. 'So what exactly am I supposed to have said? Buy me a meal and I'll give you a kiss?' Her fists clenched into hard knots. She pounded her own forehead with them, turning her face upwards to the sky. 'You are beyond belief...' she moaned.

'Am I? I took you to that banquet and you repaid me handsomely with kisses, as I remember. And as for spelling it out, you said,' he continued harshly, 'that you had a system which kept you happy. Figure out the limits, and see what can be squeezed out of them... Well, I'm afraid, being half romantic Hungarian and half blunt northerner, I don't like that kind of thing. Oh, I've seen it in action in London, time and again, of course. The clubs and parties I go to are full of girls playing those games. Usually, they have the nouse to be a bit more subtle about it, though.'

She punched one of her fists against his upper arm. His muscles were iron-hard. Her hand just bounced off. His own fists must be knotted hard inside his trouser pockets. 'You hypocrite!' she shouted. '*You* go to those clubs and parties all the time. But I steer well clear of them. If either of us is involved in that way of life, then it's *you*. It never even occurred to me when you offered to buy me a dress that really you were trying to buy *me*! I turned down your offer because I found it condescending and offensive. And all I meant by saying that I try to recognise the limits was that I try not to let life get me down.'

'Really?' He sounded both condescending and offensive now.

'Yes, really. What on earth have I done to make you think otherwise?'

There was a brief silence, then he said coldly, 'Ferry, you wouldn't come out with me when there was nothing more on offer than a quick drink in a wine-bar.'

She stopped walking and stared at him, appalled.

'I wouldn't come out with you because you were . . . were . . .'

'Were what?'

'An arrogant pig!' she bit out. 'And you still are.'

He met her eyes frostily. 'Why are you getting so angry, Ferry?' he asked.

The blue light bathed him in ice. Just minutes earlier she had looked at him, big and powerful, stretching his arms high above his head, and had felt that he was flawless. An idol. Suddenly the full force of her anger gathered beneath her breastbone like a mass of rapidly cooling lava. 'I'm angry,' she returned, her voice quaking, 'because *you* are making me angry. Oh, all that stuff about expecting sexual favours in return for jobs and goulashes and bottles of champagne is just so *predictable*. You've turned your back on everything worthwhile in your life, and instead you splash around in your materialistic, greedy lifestyle down in London, and now you've become so horribly corrupt that you can't even see straight.'

'I can't see straight?' he queried incredulously. 'If only that were true! I'd like nothing better than to become blind to your calculating wiles.'

The anger which churned inside Ferry was getting wilder and more out of control by the minute. She could hardly bring herself to believe what she was hearing. And *today* of all days. Back there in the plant he had been . . . wonderful . . . magnificent . . . She was in love with him so profoundly that it hurt. And to her horror she was discovering that, no matter how harsh and cruel his words, that feeling was every bit as potent. She loved him, and in doing so she had given him the power to hurt her beyond belief. She felt ragged and bloody inside with the pain of it. Was this how her mother had felt all those years, behind the smiles?

'How do I get to the station?' she pleaded at last, unable to face any more.

'You don't. You're staying up here with me.'

'I'm not. I can sort out my notes in the morning and fax them straight through to you.'

They were approaching the office building now. Stefan's car could be seen, all alone, in the gloom of the car park.

'No, you won't. You're staying with me.'

'You told me in Hungary that you don't force yourself on anyone!' she returned bitterly.

'I am not forcing myself on *you*,' he said, his lips thin and hard. 'I am forcing *you* on *me*. If you keep on behaving in this mendacious fashion I shall soon be cured of you. Which can only be to the good.'

'Cured of me? You make me sound like a disease.'

'You are. A nasty little virus which has burrowed into my system. I'm keeping you with me in the hope that you'll act as an antidote to your own poison.'

'You're mad!'

'I am well aware of that.'

'Take me to the station.'

'No.'

They were at the car by now. Stefan opened the passenger door, then with one, fluid, decisive movement picked her up and flung her in. He slammed the door, went round to the other side and got swiftly behind the wheel.

'Let me out.'

'No.'

'Why?'

'I've already explained that. I shall make sure you keep working for me for just as long as it takes.'

'I don't want to be your secretary. I can't imagine why you should think that I do.'

Stefan folded his arms across the wheel, sighing heavily. 'The deal's the same as it was for Rosa. It's the best you'll get.'

'What?' Ferry almost shrieked the word. 'You mean I get to be taken to bed by you and strung along by you as well? Terrific!'

Stefan started the car, looking over his shoulder as he reversed the car out of the parking bay. Then he let out a short, bitter laugh. 'That wasn't written into Rosa's contract. But I'll certainly write it into yours if you like. It should kill two birds with one stone very effectively.'

If he hadn't been driving Ferry would have attacked him with her bare fists. 'You must be crazy. Poor Rosa. I feel really sorry for her. Does she know that you cheat on her?'

'I've never had anything but a straightforward working relationship with Rosa, so I could hardly cheat on her.'

'Huh! You got to the stage of planning marriage! Do you call that a straightforward working relationship?'

There was a silence. She felt Stefan's eyes flicker back and forth from her face to the road ahead. 'What did you say?' he growled softly at length.

'There's no point in denying it. You had your office window open. So did I. I couldn't help overhearing you.'

There was another threatening silence. Then Stefan said, 'Well, well . . . So all this time you've been thinking that I had something going with Rosa . . .'

He lapsed into an even deeper silence. Ferry felt horribly unnerved. He was acting as if *she'd* got it wrong. It was a trick. It had to be because she'd heard him. And now that stupid heart of hers was jumping up and down, and, despite all the horrible things he'd said and thought about her, hope was leaping in her throat. She pinched her freckled wrist very, very hard and pressed her lips tight together. At last she could bear neither the silence nor the turmoil inside her head any longer. 'Ray *told* me she was in love with you. It's been common knowledge for months. He said that was why you sacked her.'

The silence continued. Then Stefan huffed out a huge breath between his clenched teeth. 'Tracey,' he said. 'I'll bet he was talking about Tracey. She used to slip Valentine cards into my in-tray every day of the year. She left me little notes. On the day I sacked her she'd jumped out from behind her desk and tried to plant a smacker on my cheek. I had to sack her. It had got beyond a joke. It wasn't fair on the poor kid.'

Now the silence was mutual. Forlorn hope filled Ferry's throat and her eyes until she was sure she would cry. 'Just because' and 'just because' didn't meant anything at all. He loathed her. He was lying. He simply wanted to prove a point. Crying would be the worst thing she could possibly do. 'It doesn't alter the fact that Rosa and you were discussing marriage.'

'If you know so much about Rosa's job then you'll know why. The file was in the navy cabinet all the time you were working there. Stop acting the innocent.'

'I don't know anything about Rosa's job, as it happens. Was it part of her job to propose marriage to you at regular intervals?'

More silence. 'You *must* know about Rosa's job. That's why you want it so much.'

'I *don't* want it! I told you within minutes of meeting you that I'm frequently offered permanent jobs but I never take them. Why do you keep thinking that I'm after Rosa's job?'

'You were jealous of her in Hungary. Don't deny it. I could tell. I suppose that's why you worked for Angela's agency and not anybody else's. You got jobs with all the top people. Soner or later you were bound to find

yourself a really good little niche. After all, you're far
too sharp a woman to want to go on temping all your
life. It doesn't make sense.'

'You're wrong. I never wanted a career-type job.'

He shrugged. 'Then you were using temping to find
yourself rich boyfriends.'

'Rubbish! I had plenty of boyfriends,' she muttered
angrily. 'I didn't need to go looking for them.'

'Oh, yes. That guy at the university and dear old
Gerry. Both of whom seem to have ended up feeling very
badly used. Try explaining that one, Ferry...'

Ferry closed her eyes. She wouldn't cry. It would be
too shaming. She glanced across at him. She couldn't
still love him, could she? She did.

He sighed heftily. The car was leaving the last of the
suburbs behind. The street-lights were faint and spas-
modic. Ahead of them lay blackness.

'Well, if you don't want Rosa's job, what the hell *do*
you want?'

It was pointless trying to explain anything to him. 'I
want to know why she was expecting to marry you as
well as translate your rotten correspondence,' she asked
gloomily. She might as well try to get to the bottom of
his lies. It might help, in the years to come.

He sighed again. 'I was training her to take over as
manager in London. But unfortunately my dear mother
was interfering. She wanted that end run by a member
of the family—especially as there's a seat on the board
that goes with the job. Rosa suggested a marriage of
convenience, just to keep her quiet.'

'You mean your mother...? I'm sorry, I don't understand. I find it hard to believe that your mother has much
influence in your life.'

He gave a caustic laugh. 'Little do you know. If it
weren't for her I'd have sold off the Bond Street end

years ago. All that opulent tableware isn't my style at
all. It's a shameful thing to admit, but I can't seem to
feel that it's very important. Oh, not that I don't do my
best for it—as you should know. All those ghastly
lunches with all those silly débutantes busy writing their
wedding-lists…Kumquat and Melinda, or whatever their
silly names were. Yuck…' He sighed regretfully. 'Rosa
was really good at buttering up clients… It isn't my style
at all, but she loved the social life that went with it all.
It used to drive me mad when she took her leave en-
titlement.' He snorted. '*Batteries* in the *knife* handles…'
he muttered. Then he shook his head.

She wasn't going to believe him. It would make falling
out of love so very much harder. It was bound to.
Anyway, she didn't have to. His story didn't even fit the
facts. 'Stefan, forgive me for mentioning it, but while I
was working in the office I cancelled three social en-
gagements for you with your mother. You don't exactly
give the impression of being under her thumb.'

Stefan sighed another of his leaden sighs. 'I'm not.
But it's only a couple of years since my father died.
Mother needs to keep herself occupied, and she's fixed
on the Bond Street business as her baby. You see, she
met my father in the shop. He was there on some business
concerning the Sheffield plate factory, and Mother was
a sixteen-year-old, newly arrived from Budapest, trying
to interest the proprietors in buying some pieces of silver
she had brought with her. It was love at first sight. They
got married in a matter of weeks. The first thing my
father did after getting married was to buy the business
as a sort of grand, romantic gesture. He said it was for
her…to remind her… Oh, you know the sort of stuff.
Anyway, I can hardly sell the business, now can I? But
until I can find someone of whom Mother approves to
run it I'm stuck with the job. Which was why I gave

Rosa a second and then a third chance. I couldn't bear the idea of going back to square one and being stuck in London for another year or so.'

'I see,' said Ferry greyly. 'And now you want me to take over where Rosa left off. You want to train me as the manager.' So that you can get back to the sharp side in Sheffield and have as little to do with me as possible, she added silently.

'Ferry, I can't think of anything I'd like less. But if that's the price, then I'm willing to pay it.'

The price of what? She dared not let her thoughts even consider the question... 'So who's sleeping in your bed if it isn't Rosa?' she asked sharply.

'My mother.'

'Pardon?'

'Oh, she spends half her life swanning off to London. She loves it there. I keep booking her into Claridge's, but she keeps ending up at my place. She gets lonely. I don't mind exactly; it's just that I have to run the Sheffield operation—which, as you can see from today, takes quite a bit of running—at a distance. I like to work at home in the evenings. The mobile phone and the fax machine have just about made it possible, but it's hard work none the less. Mother's presence is a bit intrusive. That's why I got that iron staircase fitted, hoping she'd take the hint without my having to be unkind. But she got herself a pair of those fold-up slippers to carry in her handbag. You should see the shoes she usually wears!'

'No wonder she's got bunions,' Ferry found herself murmuring. She swallowed hard. So he *was* flawless, after all. Oh, dear.

There was a silence. The car was driving through open countryside. The sweep of the headlights picked out

hedgerows and farm gates. Inside the car it was very
dark. There was only just enough light to make out
Stefan's profile. She looked away. She wouldn't let
herself cry.

CHAPTER TEN

STEFAN'S family home was approached by a broad gravel driveway. It was Victorian, and, as Ray had said, a proper mansion. He parked in front of the porticoed and pillared doorway, and stretched before he got out. Then he leant across to the back seat and lifted out Ferry's case.

'What happened?' he said acidly. 'Did the good stuff get pinched in Crete?'

She tried to slam her car door, but it was too well engineered. It just clunked neatly. 'No. The blue bags are my mother's.'

'Your mother's?' He didn't sound as if he believed her.

'Yes. The blue leather bags which I took to Hungary with me belong to my mother. I borrowed them. They were not bought for me by a poor sap in return for a peck on the cheek. If you like I can ask my mother if she still has the receipts. It's possible. She's very methodical.'

'But I thought your mother was... At least, you said that she had to struggle...'

'My mother was a student when I was a child. She is now a senior partner with the solicitors Morgan, Freeman——'

'And Lyon?' he groaned.

'That's right.'

'I'm impressed.'

'Why? Because she can afford to buy her own luggage?' Ferry snapped sarcastically. 'Good grief,

Stefan. You do surprise me... Fancy being impressed
because you hear of a woman who pays her own way in
the world. You must be moving in the wrong circles...'

'For goodness' sake, Ferry, haven't you listened to
anything I've said? I don't like all those clubs and parties
I have to go to. It's strictly business as far as I'm concerned. Anyway, how was I to know that your mother
was so successful?'

'You just pigeon-holed her, I suppose.'

He thought for a moment. When he spoke he sounded
unaccustomedly serious. 'I don't know. Perhaps I did.
You told me that she had a struggle to bring you up and
that her Christmas decorations were tatty. It...it didn't
exactly conjure up a picture in my mind of a top contract lawyer.'

Ferry glared at him. 'So simply because you didn't
know my mother was successful you chose to think that
I'd inveigled someone into buying me the bags?'

'Can we drop the subject?'

Ferry shook her head. 'That night—at the banquet.
My coat and dress and the diamonds...they were gifts
from my parents. Did you think I'd accepted those in
return for...favours, too?'

'Leave it, Ferry!' growled Stefan irritably. Then he
turned his back on her and marched up to the front door,
suitcase in hand. He fished in his pocket for his keys
and opened the door.

'Are you coming?' he asked crossly, standing in the
doorway, looking back at her over his shoulder.

'Of course,' she said archly, following him inside. 'You
haven't left me much choice. Nor have you answered my
question.'

'OK,' he returned angrily, slamming the door and then
leaning against it. 'I don't really know what I thought.
I knew how much I paid Angela for your services. And

I knew that Angela would take her cut before passing the residue on to you. It was OK, as salaries for temps go. Quite good in fact. But there was no way that it would stretch to the sort of clothes you were wearing— especially as you wore such smart clothes to work. I mean, it wasn't as if you made do with cheap stuff for work and then blew all your money on a couple of good things for special occasions.'

'So you spent the whole evening totting up the price of the clothes on my back? Well, well...'

'No! I didn't even start thinking about it till later...'

'Oh. I see. You saved it for when you were kissing me? Your mouth was occupied, but it left your brain free to undertake a little mental arithmetic. I'm charmed.'

'Damn it, Ferry! Both of us were involved in that kiss. I don't know about you—though I can guess from the way you responded—but *my* mind was in no fit state to think anything at all. It had turned to volcanic ash.'

Ferry folded her arms and looked down at her feet. She really didn't want to be reminded of that kiss. 'So just exactly when did you do your miscalculations?' she asked sourly.

'Oh... look, Ferry. I got it wrong. I admit it. But it seemed to make sense. Gerry said something, and I thought... And then that kiss was so unbelievably erotic that I thought, Damn it, the man's a complete imbecile! And then afterwards you just froze me off. I thought, How the hell can she be kissing me like that one minute and then running for cover the next? It didn't make sense. I was angry. Even when we got in my car I thought something really good had started between us, and then you got out your pencil and offered to take dictation. Dictation! I just couldn't believe my ears. Until I saw your flat, that was. It's *superb*, and it isn't even as if you share it with a couple of other girls...' He ran one hand angrily through his hair, and shook his head. 'What was I supposed to think?'

'The flat,' she said through lips white with anger, 'was a seventeenth-birthday present from my mother. When she saw that I didn't want to leave home like other girls, she had the ground floor converted for me. Unlike *your* mother, my mother had plenty to occupy her. I haven't found it exactly plain sailing having a mother so dedicated to her career. I had no desire to end up like her.'

And I still don't, she found herself thinking mournfully. Twenty-five years was an awfully long time, even if it had come right in the end.

He shrugged. 'OK...' he conceded cagily. 'I've already admitted that I got you wrong. Badly wrong. So I apologise.' He didn't sound as if he meant it.

'Thank you.' She didn't sound as if she meant it, either.

There was a horrible silence, during which they both stood facing each other. Stefan's eyes were sharp and accusing. Ferry's blazed with fury.

So that was what Stefan bloody Redwell had thought of her. He thought she was a scheming little gold-digger who was feathering her nest at the expense of well-heeled boyfriends, found through her temping assignments. And she was so pathetically stupid that she *still* loved him, and would probably still be hankering after him twenty-five years from now.

The hall was very large, with a black and white tiled floor. It was so large that a gleaming black concert grand piano occupied a mere quarter of the space. Ferry walked stiffly over to it and raised the lid. Stefan stormed to the other end of the hall and began opening doors and snapping on lights.

She stroked the keys. They felt soothing beneath her fingertips. Then she played middle C. Even she could tell that the tone was beautiful.

Stefan came to stand beside her. 'Do you play?' he asked brusquely.

She looked steadily at him. 'You should know the answer to that by now. I do *not* play.'

He put his hands on his hips and stared at her very steadily. 'Ferry, I've apologised once. I'm certainly not going to do it again.'

'You thought such dreadful things about me, Stefan,' she burst out. 'How could you?'

And then Stefan's eyes caught fire again. 'So *what*? You thought dreadful things about me. You jumped straight to the conclusion that I had something going with those awful debs. OK, I didn't put you straight because I hoped it might get you jealous... But I didn't know you thought I was going to marry *Rosa*. You just assumed I'd cheat on her without giving it a second thought! *And* you thought that I didn't give a damn about my work. You thought——'

'OK, OK,' she bellowed across his accusing words. Oh, damn him! He was right! There was nothing to choose between them when all was said and done. She put her hands on her hips and shouted, 'Well, I apologise too!'

'Well, thank you very much!' roared Stefan ungraciously.

She slapped her hand down on the piano keys, so that an ear-splitting discord rent the air.

He grabbed hold of her wrist. 'Stop it!' he ordered. 'You'll wake the whole house.'

'But you said there was no one here. Just one more of your lies, huh?'

'The dogs... you'll start the dogs off.'

Uncannily, the dogs chose that moment to acknowledge their presence. Somewhere in the depths of the house they set up a dreadful howling.

Ferry glowered furiously. Stefan scowled just as angrily. And then, together, grimly, they started to laugh.

Furiously Ferry put out a hand and pushed Stefan very hard in the chest. 'You did that on purpose, didn't you? You made the dogs do that so I'd start laughing. I hate you!' she cried. 'I don't want to laugh with you. Stop them barking... Stop them...' Her words dissolved into helpless laughter.

Stefan stopped laughing. He stood very still for a moment, and then he caught hold of both her wrists and pulled her against him. 'First,' he said, 'you can answer a few questions.'

'No,' she said, shaking her head and fighting the stupid, almost hysterical laughter which shook her from top to bottom. The dogs howled even louder. She collapsed against his big frame. With his hands encircling her wrists, his breath warm against her cheek and the sensation of his muscular body hard against her, she suddenly found that she didn't want to laugh at all any more. She stopped as abruptly as she had started. Frantically she tried to wrestle herself away from him, but he held her tight, looping one arm around her so that she was crushed against him.

And then their eyes clashed and his lips parted, showing the glint of his strong white teeth. A muscle flickered in his cheek. She heard him draw in a sharp, deep breath. And then he started to kiss her. She was totally lost from the moment his firm lips caught hungrily at hers. Her mouth opened swiftly, letting his tongue explore the moist contours of her own. It was everything she remembered, and yet shockingly different.

All that frightened, tamped desire surged u̧
whelm her as they kissed. It filled her, roaring into
and crevices, while his mouth pounded hers with its
gency. Her skin prickled from top to toe. Her round,
full breasts hardened with it, and grew heavy with it. Her
blood carried it, sharp and sweet, needling out its
presence in every corner of her being. She fell against
him, letting her flesh rock against his, while their mouths
melded; moved; gnawed at the very essence of the other.

His hands came to hold her head, one each side,
holding it as a man raging with thirst might hold a gourd,
hard against his mouth. Then one hand freed itself and
came to rest on her shoulder, biting against her skin. His
fingerpads dug deep against muscle and bone, and then
moved fervently down her upper arm and across to cup
her breast. She could feel his hand dragging against her
skin, moving desperately towards its mark, and she ached
for it. She squirmed and thrust her breast against his
open palm.

His fingers closed, kneading her flesh through her
clothes, his thumb discovering the engorged point of her
nipple and drawing such pangs of pleasure from it that
she could hardly breathe. Round and round his thumb
moved, until her nipple stood so proud and tugged so
hard on that molten core of desire deep inside her that
she almost hurt with the power of her arousal. At last
her craving body began to shake and shudder with the
sweet ache of wanting him. It was more than she could
bear. She had to draw back a little—either that or cry
out loud, and her mouth refused to forsake the embrace
which silenced it.

His movements became more gentle then. He flat-
tened his hand against her pliant flesh and caressed it
tenderly. Eased, she closed on him, and let her pleasure
flow from the lightness of his touch. They seemed almost

ʌe one person, moving and holding and rocking in such a sweet unison, each responding to the nuances of the other's flesh. Ferry moaned helplessly in the back of her throat. Oh, this was the kiss he had promised that night, when his lips had first met hers. This was the kiss that she had fought against. Her body had rushed to embrace this promise every single time she had been with him; but until now she had pummelled and punched and squeezed her burgeoning desire into surrender.

Now her senses would not be constrained. They knew what they wanted and they would have it. Denied so often, they now carried her with such a swift urgency that her control slipped away. Her hands fell to grasp the muscle of his hips and clenched tight, pleading silently for everything he had to give.

He let his mouth fall away from hers, the coarse barb of his chin grazing her cheek. He breathed for a moment, shudderingly, his mouth resting against her hair.

Then he said in a voice low and thick with desire, '*Now* we will make love properly. I shall take you upstairs to my apartment and I will take off all your clothes, and, naked, we will make love.'

Ferry began to tremble. She wanted to say yes but she couldn't speak. The tremor took hold of her, until she had to clench her jaw to stop her teeth chattering. She was burningly hot, like someone gripped by a fever. And her unassuaged hunger was painful to her untutored flesh.

'You're not going to say no,' he ground out fiercely.

Still she could make no reply. All that strong, crashing emotion which had been encased in chicken wire for all those years had spilled free. Now it poured into her mind, drowning all thought in a torrent of pure feeling. She loved him so. She needed him. No matter what he felt, her own feelings had seethed out of control. She must have him.

'God, Ferraleth ... don't say no ...' he pleaded.

She tried to say yes, but only anguished breath escaped her throat. She bit her teeth together again.

'Tell me ... Tell me you will ...'

But still no words would come. Her body was thundering with desire. It crackled through her with a violence that shocked her. Of course she would make love with him. *Of course*. In her mind and her mouth was only love. Pure love ... *Of course*. It was singing, and crying and weeping and exulting and rejoicing. She *loved* him. It was much, much better than being empty inside. It filled her until she felt she must burst. Why couldn't she tell him that she would go with him? Why couldn't she say that one, liberating word?

He stared down at her for a long moment. She tried to nod but the muscles in her neck had locked rigid. Her shoulders bunched upwards with a convulsive shudder.

'You want me,' he said tenderly at last, his eyes seeming to shimmer like molten gold, and he swallowed so hard that his Adam's apple moved sharply beneath his jutting chin.

Very slowly, very gently, as if soothing someone injured and shocked, he said, 'I'm going to carry you upstairs, Ferraleth. I'm going to lay you on my bed. And then I'm going to get us both undressed, and I'm going to kiss you again and again and again ...'

Her swollen lips stayed parted. They felt bruised and dry. Her eyes wouldn't focus. She could almost hear the pleasure of her body, whispering inside. She clenched her stomach muscles and felt its source, like a hard, solid thing, low down, pulsing out its need: wave upon wave of thrilling pleasure, rippling outwards, pleading for release.

One hand came round beneath her arms and brushed against her breast. The other hand dipped to her knees, and suddenly she was swinging up through the air, lifted securely by the iron-hard muscles of Stefan, her cheek, warm and dry and eager, heavy against his chest. She heard his heart beat steadily as he moved towards the stairs. She felt his breath on her skin. She smelled his smell. Limp now, her taut muscles eased by his certainty, she curled against him and waited. He laid her on the bed, as he had promised he would.

The bed was not a lovers' bed. It was covered with a rough plaid rug in tawny browns and golds. The cloth prickled against her skin. It felt like...like him... She didn't know it but she smiled as he took off her shoes. She continued to smile, just faintly and sweetly and honestly as he fumbled her buttons with his big square fingers. All the time she watched him. His hair fell untidily forward. The lines on his face eased away. His nostrils quivered slightly as he took in breath after breath. At last, her own breasts surging before her eyes as she breathed in and out, she saw him reveal his own self. The hasty impatience with which she had so often seen him discard his clothes was set aside. Slowly he peeled off his waistcoat, sitting protectively beside her. He unbuttoned his cuffs, and then his shirt-front, and let the damp cotton slide haltingly away from his broad, powerful shoulders. She saw the hollows of his collarbone appear and disappear. She saw the dense, curling hairs on his muscular chest become erect, like a golden cloud over his skin. She saw his flat, male nipples, paler than her own, prickle into sensitive nubs. He was naked at last, and she saw his flesh desire her.

He knelt beside her on the bed. Then he lowered his head and kissed her lips, very breathily and very gently. Her dry lips parted to him, eager to taste the quiet pace of adoration. Her wide-set grey eyes stayed open, half shadowed by her eyelids, absorbing every inch of his massive, powerfully built body. At last she saw his thighs, strong and hard, coming to straddle her as his mouth bent to claim first one breast and then the other. She lifted her heavy, languorous hands to his shoulders, and let her fingers rumple that thick, corn-ripe hair, while he drew one hard brown nipple into his mouth.

The mobile pressure of his tongue stirred against her skin. For both of them it signalled a fresh rhythm. Again her need mounted, fierce and demanding, so that she arched against him, shuddering with pleasure.

At last he threw back his head and groaned. She watched the muscles of his neck cord tight. 'I— uh——' he said, and he stopped to release a ragged sigh.

Then, 'I can't wait, Ferraleth,' he said painfully. 'But if I must, I will. If you tell me, I will...'

His hands were close to her shoulders and she felt them knot into fists as he took his weight on his forearms and leaned over her, gazing into her eyes. 'Don't make me...' he pleaded thickly.

She found her voice. 'Don't wait,' she whispered. There was a brief pause, and then with a great cry of joy his flesh joined hers at last.

Deep inside her, he froze. His arms strained as he lifted his face high. 'My God, Ferraleth,' he moaned. 'Why in heaven's name didn't you tell me you were a virgin?'

'I...' Oh, this felt so good. The sharp, sweet pain had gone. She was moist and ready and aching for him. She felt her dark centre close around him. Her legs clenched against his hips, urging him. 'It wasn't important,' she murmured. 'Please, Stefan... I want you...'

Still he remained frozen, his muscles taut, sweat breaking on his skin. 'I know what you were waiting for now,' he groaned, as if a great pain was bursting inside him. 'It was marriage. Our marriage. This marriage. Oh, God, I love you, Ferraleth,' and he began to thrust then, beyond reason, driven by instincts too powerful to control.

She moved with him. Intuitively, but at first awkwardly, and then suddenly with a fluent ease; and all the while gasping with an excitement which mounted so compellingly that she was bewildered. It was only when ecstasy had flooded through her, freezing her in its power, blinding all her senses into a thrilling oblivion, that she understood.

He was with her. He lay heavily across her, his skin damp against hers, his breath mingling with hers. She laid her hands flat on his back and ran her tongue gently across his shoulder. They were one person. He loved her, and they had made themselves one. Time passed. At last he untangled his limbs from hers and rolled over on his back.

'I love you,' he said drowsily. 'You will marry me, won't you?'

'Yes.'

'I expect we'll argue all the time.'

'Yes.'

'It'll be nice, though, won't it?'

'Yes.'

He propped himself up on one elbow and looked down at her. 'So you are good at saying yes, after all,' he laughed.

She shook her head. 'Not any more. I've re-thought my philosophy of life.'

'You mean you don't want to try to be happy?'

'No. Why should I? I *am* happy. I don't need to try any more.'

Stefan reached up one hand and rumpled his hair. 'You've nearly driven me around the bend. You're very perverse.'

'Me!' she exclaimed, sitting up and hugging her knees to her chest. 'You are the most perverse——'

He shook his head. 'I am not perverse. I saw you and I thought you were terrific, and then I straight away started to fall in love with you and I asked you out. What's perverse about that?'

Ferry blinked. 'Did you?' she muttered, astonished.

'Yes,' he said. 'And you felt exactly the same. I could tell. So tell me,' he continued dangerously, 'just tell me why you wouldn't come out with me that first day. It was there from the first moment . . . wasn't it? You know that as well as I do. I took one look at you, and you sat at that desk and looked up at me from under your fringe, and it was all so damned obvious! And then all day long it was the same. All that stuff about the Russian letters— I wanted to shout out loud with delight. We spent the whole day knocking sparks off one another, didn't we? It had never happened to me before. I couldn't believe it. It was fantastic. And then I told you how beautiful your name was, and you said that it was more beautiful than you were, and I just looked at you and I thought, *Nothing* is more beautiful than that face. And then . . . then you didn't go home at five o'clock and I was so *sure* . . . So I asked. And you wouldn't come. Why?'

'I . . .' Ferry looked up at him, very meekly from beneath her fringe. 'I haven't a clue why I didn't go out with you that first day,' she murmured, genuinely baffled. 'I must have been mad. You're right. It was terribly, devastatingly obvious . . . wasn't it?'

He rested his lips against her temple. 'Yes,' he said.

'Then . . . then why didn't you ask me out again?'

Now it was Stefan's turn to look baffled. 'Pride, probably,' he said, pulling a puzzled face. 'And that smile of yours. It was like a brick wall. We seemed to get locked into mortal combat, didn't we? Though I have to admit that I was getting pretty desperate by the Friday. That was why I wangled the invitation to that dreadful banquet... I was determined you shouldn't find an excuse for not coming. That was why I offered the dress and everything...'

'The steak was tough,' said Ferry blankly. Then she added, 'I can't think any more...'

Stefan let his mouth travel across her brow and then obliquely across her cheek towards her mouth. 'Nor can I,' he murmured. 'I can't imagine how you could think I was—um——' His firm lips nibbled lightly at her skin. She slipped her free hand to the back of his neck and let her fingers trickle through his hair.

'Doing sums...' she whispered mindlessly.

'Hnngg...'

He'd said that once before. When he had a pencil in his mouth. She remembered that. Oddly enough, she remembered everything he'd ever said to her. Only this time he couldn't speak because his mouth was covering hers and he was kissing her properly. This time, though, she didn't urge him ever faster. He had promised once to be a very attentive lover. As her desire unfolded once more for him, she lay bonelessly on the pillows and allowed him to prove his pledge. She wasn't disappointed. Slowly, and with the greatest of delicacy, he carried her sensations along a much gentler, winding path to the same ecstatic destination.

She didn't remember him rolling off her, to lie, damp and replete, on the sheet. A fuzzy, animal sleep had come to claim her, carrying her from the black pool of newly satisfied desire to the dark sea of the night. When next she became conscious of him it was morning, and he was sleeping still. One golden, sinewy arm lay flung across her. She blinked into the face of his Rolex and sighed. It was almost ten o'clock.

Happily she nudged him awake. Happily she watched his eyes open and then blink slowly, as if they, too, couldn't quite encompass the truth. Two of a kind, pillowed in love, they reached out and soothed each other's brows. 'I love you,' they whispered together, and then they laughed.

'All those freckles...' he said lovingly. 'I'm going to kiss every one of them.'

'Do you like them?'

'Mmm. They make you look like a——'

'Don't tell me. A speckled egg.'

'An egg? What a funny idea. You're quite the wrong shape for an egg.' He leaned back on one elbow and let his gaze travel slowly from her head right down to her toes. 'Those wonderful long legs,' he sighed. 'Just like a Dalmatian.'

'Oh, Stefan,' she laughed. 'You Hungarians are so romantic!'

He frowned. 'I'll call you my little speckled egg if you like.'

'No. Don't.'

'Good. Because I want to call you Ferraleth. It's the most beautiful name I've ever heard.'

She smiled happily. 'Shall I call you István, then?' she giggled.

He slumped back down on the pillows. 'Try not to,' he said wryly. 'It reminds me too much of my mother.'

'Oh, dear. Is she going to be a problem?'

He sighed. 'I hope not. But she did rather have an Eastern European princess in mind for me.'

'We can tell her my father's a Dalmatian, if you like. I get my freckles from him, you know.'

Stefan smiled broadly. 'Good thinking, Ferraleth. *Now* all you have to do is to think of a way of getting her out of my hair in every other respect.'

'That's easy,' smiled Ferraleth. 'Let her run the London office herself. She's so charming. She'd do all the sucking up brilliantly, and she doesn't put people's backs up, either. Ray thinks the world of her.'

Stefan's smile grew even broader. 'Brilliant! I can always get an efficient manager to advise her on business matters. Why didn't I think of it myself?'

'Pigeon-holes,' said Ferraleth bluntly.

He nodded ruefully, then reached out one muscular arm to the phone beside his bed. He tapped out a few numbers.

'Candice... Yes. I know I'm late... Not for hours and hours, I shouldn't think...'

Ferry frowned at him. Fancy making a business call at a time like this. Well, she wasn't going to make it easy for him. She leaned across him and let her mouth brush the golden hairs on his arm. Gently she ran her lips up and down his arm. It was unbelievably erotic. She did it again. He flinched. He closed his eyes and bit his lip.

Then he took a deep breath. 'Did it?' he said into the receiver. 'Good. Great. Look, Candice, there's something I want you to do for me. Find a firm to put rubber treads on the staircase to my London flat. Yes. That's right. Bye...'

And then he slammed down the phone and rolled over. 'Lie on your stomach,' he ordered.

'Why?'

'I'm going to kiss all those freckles. Starting with the ones on your... hnngg...'

Ferry shivered with delight. There were so many of them. This was going to take an awfully long time...

Full of Eastern Passion...

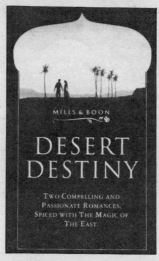

Savour the romance of the East this summer with
our two full-length compelling Romances,
wrapped together in one exciting volume.

AVAILABLE FROM 29 JULY 1994   PRICED £3.99

MILLS & BOON

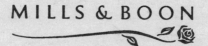

4 FREE

Romances and 2 FREE gifts just for you!

You can enjoy all the heartwarming emotion of true love for FREE! Discover the heartbreak and happiness, the emotion and the tenderness of the modern relationships in Mills & Boon Romances.

We'll send you 4 Romances as a special offer from Mills & Boon Reader Service, along with the opportunity to have 6 captivating new Romances delivered to your door each month.

Claim your FREE books and gifts overleaf...

An irresistible offer from Mills & Boon

Become a regular reader of Romances with Mills & Boon Reader Service and we'll welcome you with 4 books, a CUDDLY TEDDY and a special MYSTERY GIFT all absolutely FREE.

And then look forward to receiving 6 brand new Romances each month, delivered to your door hot off the presses, postage and packing FREE! Plus our free Newsletter featuring author news, competitions, special offers and much more.

This invitation comes with no strings attached. You may cancel or suspend your subscription at any time, and still keep your free books and gifts.

It's so easy. Send no money now. Simply fill in the coupon below and post it to -
Reader Service, FREEPOST, PO Box 236, Croydon, Surrey CR9 9EL.

NO STAMP REQUIRED
Free Books Coupon

Yes! Please rush me 4 FREE Romances and 2 FREE gifts! Please also reserve me a Reader Service subscription. If I decide to subscribe I can look forward to receiving 6 brand new Romances for just £11.40 each month, postage and packing FREE. If I decide not to subscribe I shall write to you within 10 days - I can keep the free books and gifts whatever I choose. I may cancel or suspend my subscription at any time. I am over 18 years of age.

Ms/Mrs/Miss/Mr _____ EP71R

Address _____

_____

Postcode _____ Signature _____

mps
MAILING
PREFERENCE
SERVICE